Young Heroes of Gettysburg

By
William Thomas Venner

WM™ KIDS 10 WHITE MANE KIDS

This White Mane Books publication
was printed by
Beidel Printing House, Inc.
63 West Burd Street
Shippensburg, PA 17257-0152 USA

In respect for the scholarship contained herein, the acid-free paper used in this book meets the guidelines for permanence and durability of the Committee on Production Guidelines for Book Longevity of the Council on Library Resources.

For a complete list of available publications
please write
White Mane Books
Division of White Mane Publishing Company, Inc.
P.O. Box 152
Shippensburg, PA 17257-0152 USA

Library of Congress Cataloging-in-Publication Data

Venner, William Thomas, 1950-
   Young heroes of Gettysburg / by William Thomas Venner.
       p. cm.
   Includes bibliographical references.
   Summary: Two young Indiana soldiers participate in the battle of Gettysburg; one is wounded and forced to rely on the help of two young women living in Gettysburg.
   ISBN 1-57249-200-7 (alk. paper)
   1. Gettysburg (Pa.), Battle of, 1863--Juvenile Fiction. [1. Gettysburg (Pa.), Battle of, 1863--Fiction. 2. United States--History--Civil War, 1861-1865--Fiction.] I. Title.

PZ7.V5618 Yo 2000
[Fic]--dc21

                                                                                    00-035929

To

Young Heroes of Gettysburg is dedicated to those teen-agers who know that their ancestors are nearby and watching. This book is also dedicated to some of my favorite teens: Sam and Rachel Farfsing, Nicole and Ben Ellis, Jamie Wages, and Kristy Ridler.

Contents

Illustrations

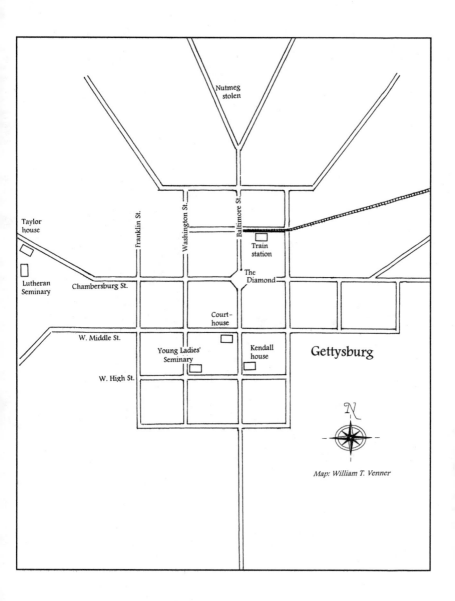

Map: William T. Venner

Chapter 1

Marching to Gettysburg

The early morning sky was just light enough for the three boys to see where they were going. Johnny Baker, Ben Ellis, and Sam Bradshaw crept quietly past a large stone barn and followed a path leading towards the farm's chicken coops. The boys' timing was perfect, there was enough light to see, but not enough to wake the chickens. Therefore, the birds slumbered peacefully, not knowing that thieves were approaching.

Sixteen-year-old Johnny led the way, followed by his close friends. The three boys were soldiers, members of Colonel Williams' 19th Indiana regiment. For the past two years they had been marching and fighting across Virginia and Maryland. Though the Union army fed the boys sufficient quantities of salt pork, beans, rice, and hardtack, they still preferred the taste of fresh chicken. Thus, the three experienced chicken thieves slipped noiselessly into the pungent-smelling chicken coop and hastily stuffed four chickens into a gunnysack.

The foragers retreated from the chicken coop and retraced their steps back towards the barn. However, the boys' escape was not going to be easy. The farmer's dogs picked up the soldiers' scent and came to investigate. Once the dogs determined their territory had been invaded they began to howl. The boys

Johnny Baker

William T. Venner Collection

Sam Bradshaw

William T. Venner Collection

Ben Ellis

raced past the huge stone barn, their hearts pounding in dread. The dogs took up the chase, barking excitedly, but the boys had too much of a lead. The three scampered through a garden and dashed towards a solidly made wooden-picket fence. Reaching the fence, they jumped over white-painted slats, and landed safely on the other side. The dogs halted at the fence line, yowling in frustration.

Johnny climbed to his feet, brushed the mud from his woolen uniform, and laughed at the disappointed dogs. He turned his back on the barking animals and began walking away, his soldier's boots crunching on the gravel lane. His friend, Sam, fell in right behind, lugging the gunnysack over his shoulder.

"Wait a minute," called Ben. His two friends paused and turned around. "I got to thank the farmer." Johnny and Sam groaned but did not leave. The two boys knew Ben was fastidiously honest and that whenever they took chickens, he would write a note thanking the farmer, and then would leave some money.

It only took a couple moments to write his note on a piece of cartridge paper. He reached into his pockets and took out three nickels. Ben then rolled the coins inside the paper and stuck the brown paper in a crack in a fence post. With that, Ben felt better and caught up with his friends.

"Let's get back to the company before the captain misses us."

"Who cares about the captain," laughed Sam, who feared almost nothing. The muscular youth stretched his arms and lifted the chicken-filled gunnysack high into the air, saying, "It's the first sergeant who we got to fool."

"What. Are you afraid of First Sergeant Carder?" asked Johnny, as the three hurried back to the regiment. The sun had risen now, casting long shadows. The morning was warm and smelled richly of moist earth, damp hay, and cow manure.

"No, I'm not afraid of no one," growled Sam. "It's just, if he catches us, he'll make us dig some more sinks." Ben and Johnny smiled at each other. They knew that Sam was not frightened by anything that the war had thrown at them. The youth did not tremble before the battles, as many of the soldiers did, nor did he worry about being hurt. Sam was not fearful of the regiment's officers, or the sergeants. In fact, the boys knew that Sam could almost always talk his way out of any trouble he got himself into.

Ben looked at his two friends, knowing they enjoyed baiting each other. Johnny took his big black hat from his head and wiped at the sweat that was already beginning to bead on his forehead. Ben saw Johnny's big ears sticking out prominently. There had been many a schoolboy who had made the mistake of laughing at Johnny's ears, and Sam had busted their noses and blackened their eyes. Johnny had also surprised some of the soldiers in their company who made fun of him. Those fellows, and some of them had been much larger than Johnny, quickly learned that his ears were not to be discussed.

Ben knew both of the teens seemed fearless. Johnny approached the terrors of military life just like Sam. He worried about nothing, and relished every hardship that they had encountered. But there was one difference between Johnny and Sam. Johnny did have one thing that terrorized him, and that was girls. He did not know how to speak to them, nor know how to act whenever young ladies were around. The usually self-confident youth became tongue-tied, ill-at-ease, and stood about stiffly with clammy hands, and a deeply red, blushing face.

Ben marveled at Sam's and Johnny's courage, and took comfort from his friends' stoutheartedness, but realized that he did not have their same audacity. Ben trembled before every battle, shivering from fear, regardless of how hot the summer's sun had heated the air. He struggled to keep his knees from knocking, and from shaking so badly that others could see his fear. But Ben had vowed to himself to never leave his friends' side. If they went into battle, so would Ben. He was part of the trio, and together with Sam and Johnny, the three were stalwart, self-supporting, and almost invincible.

The three boys crested a low tree-studded hill and looked down into the shallow valley below them. The 19th Indiana was camped here, next to a sluggish stream that the locals called Marsh Creek. The chicken-thieves became alarmed when they realized that nearly all of the tents had been taken down. The normal sounds made by a regiment while in camp had been replaced by the orderly commotion of noises of a battalion forming up for a road march. The youths rushed down the hill and raced to collect their gear.

Lieutenant Crockett East was waiting for them. The tall officer stroked his dark mustache and frowned at the three. "I see you have been out foraging," he said softly.

"Well, sir," began Sam, who tried to hide the gunnysack behind his back.

"No, Sammy, I don't have time to hear your excuses. The regiment is moving out any minute now. I want you boys to get all your accoutrements and fall in with the company. I'll attend to your problem when we have more time. Now, move it, lickety-split."

"Yes sir," the three said simultaneously, and saluted their officer. He turned his back on them and called for a sergeant. The youths scampered away and hurried to their gear.

As Ben was taking apart the shelter halves of their tent he remembered his dream from last night and shuddered. The young blacksmith had dreamt that the regiment would go into battle today and that his friend

Crockett East

William T. Venner Collection

would get hurt. Ben awoke from his slumber, his heart pounding and sweating profusely. He did not know if he should believe in the dream or not, but he could remember that his old Grandma Ellis had taken great stock in the meanings of dreams. Maybe, thought Ben, he should consider the dream as a warning.

"Johnny," he whispered.

Johnny was on his knees, rolling up his gray-woolen blanket. He strapped the well-worn blanket to the top of his pack and then turned to Ben. "Yep, what do you want?"

"Would you mind if I carried your half of the gear, today?" Ben wondered how strange this request would sound since the two youths had always divided up their gear, with one person carrying half, and the other getting the rest. Now, thought Ben, if the dream was correct, and something did happen to Johnny, then half of their gear might possibly be lost or stolen.

"What?" asked the puzzled Johnny.

"I was just thinking it might be nice if we changed things just a little. Today I carry everything and you get a break. Tomorrow you get to haul it all. What do you think?"

"You want to lug my stuff, as well as yours?"

"Right. It would be different," he said sheepishly.

"Yeah, I'll say." Johnny scratched at some lice and then shrugged. "Well, okay. But tomorrow I want my turn. There's no way you're going to say that Johnny doesn't carry his own load!"

"Thanks, friend," said Ben with relief. He collected Johnny's camping gear and stuffed it into his pack. Ellis stood up and adjusted the knapsack to his shoulders, already noticing the additional difference in weight. Ben wondered if he had done the right thing. The two young soldiers had learned a long time ago that by splitting the gear between themselves and each carrying half the load, both boys had made their own lives easier. Today, the added equipment would bother Ben everywhere he went. However, if there was a battle, and Johnny was actually hurt, then tomorrow, Ben would still have all of the gear.

The regimental drummers began beating the long roll, the rhythm informing the soldiers it was time to "fall in" to formation. Since the boys were some of the shorter soldiers in the unit, and the troops formed up by height, the three quickly assumed their positions near the left end of Company K. Ben looked to his right and recognized Corporal Allen Galyean. On Ben's left was Johnny, who had strapped the chicken-laden gunnysack over his shoulder. Standing right behind Ben was Sam, and behind him was Jim Benton. There were lots more fellows in Company K, and Ben knew everyone by name, and many by their behaviors, but once they were in line, Ben's world was reduced to his comrades immediately around him.

Captain William Orr stepped in front of the unit and called the company to attention. The redheaded officer then ordered them to stand at ease. The captain informed his men that the regiment would soon be marching, with their day's destination to be Gettysburg. He motioned to Lieutenant East to take charge of the company, and then wandered away, heading for a cluster of officers who had gathered around the regiment's commander, Colonel Williams.

Ben watched their captain walk towards the colonel and then turned to Johnny. "Wow, we just made it back in time."

"Yeah," answered Johnny, "have no fear when I'm in charge of a foraging expedition." He patted the lumps in the gunnysack and the unhappy fowl shifted about. "I haven't had time to wring their necks but I will when I get a chance. They'll be good eat'un tonight, a whole lot better than crackers and salt pork."

Just then Lieutenant East slid up behind the two friends and gently tapped Johnny's shoulder. "I haven't forgotten," he warned.

"What?" asked Sam innocently.

The lieutenant tapped the gunnysack with his hand and glared at him.

"Oh, you're just mad at us 'cause we drove you out of your classroom."

Lieutenant East laughed a hearty chuckle. "No Sammy, my boy, that was years ago. Back then I was your teacher. You guys were supposed to do things like that." They all laughed. Ben thought back to that day in early April 1860. He was 12 then, and a gangly, strappling of a boy. Ben was attending school in Selma, Indiana, and both Johnny and Sam were in the same class. The long cold of the winter melted away, and the constant rains of spring had ceased. The students all fretted at having to be inside as the weather had turned sunny and warm, and their very souls cried to be released to frolic and run about beneath the welcome sun. But instead, a heartless teacher who forced them to learn arithmetic held the students prisoner.

When they were released for the lunch hour Sam had an odd look on his face. Ben and Johnny knew from experience that this expression meant excitement. The youths crowded around him and he whispered his plan. Johnny and Ben shrank back in horror, but Sam kept talking and soon convinced them to help him with his scheme.

The goal was simple: they would drive the teacher from the classroom. The means for accomplishing this task had an element of danger in it, and a large promise for pain. But Sam, who already was well known for his fearlessness, told them he would handle the dangerous part. All they had to do was jam the schoolhouse windows so they could not be opened.

It only took Ben and Johnny a couple minutes to sneak back into the classroom and shove kindling into the window sashes and render them inoperative. East caught the two conspirators as they tried to slip out of the classroom. When he asked them what they had been doing, Ben could only shrug his shoulders and look down at his feet. Johnny made an attempt to come up with an excuse but was unsuccessful. The teacher chuckled at their uneasiness and warned the boys not to take up a life of crime. The two promised not to become criminals and the teacher let them go. Ben and Johnny scampered away to safety.

Meanwhile, Sam had made excellent use of the distraction. Just as soon as he saw their teacher corner his two friends Sam crept behind the teacher, carrying a large muslin sack, being mindful of the squeaking floorboards, and stole into the classroom. He placed the sack on the teacher's desk and then cautiously untied the drawstring. He immediately covered the bag with a wooden pail. Then, Sam retreated from the room, and escaped unnoticed.

At the end of the lunch hour East lined the Selma children up and marched them back into his classroom. The students sat down at their desks, the boys on the right side of the room, the girls on the left. The youths buzzed with excitement. They knew something interesting was going to happen, especially when they saw the upside-down pail sitting on the teacher's desk. The teacher approached his desk cautiously as the little children giggled behind him.

The lanky educator turned to Ben and Johnny and questioned them, but they stared down at their shoes, shrugged their shoulders, and shook their heads. East sighed, placed his hands upon the wooden pail and slowly lifted it up. A buzzing sound filled the room, and a cloud of angry hornets swarmed out from beneath the pail. The teacher quickly set the pail back down, covering the hornet's nest, but the damage had been done. Hundreds of furious yellow jackets whirled around the room.

The children began to scream and run a ing to escape the hornets' assaults. The older tried to open the windows but found them ja shut. There was nothing for the students to do escape out the front door. The teacher was the last retreat from the room, and as the red-faced teache did, he was looking for Ben, Sam, and Johnny. But the three boys had already made their getaway, and were one hundred yards down the street, already heading for home.

"Yes," said Lieutenant East, "you boys did ruin my teaching plans for the rest of the day, but it was such a fine afternoon." The officer paused for a moment, smiling. "If I remember right, wasn't that the day that everyone got horribly sunburned?" They all laughed, recalling that far-off spring afternoon down by the millpond.

"Now, be careful today," advised the boys' teacher-now-turned-lieutenant.

"There going to be a fight?" asked Johnny.

"It's possible," said East. "Colonel Williams mentioned reports of some rebels not far from Gettysburg. He didn't say how many, or what kind, but if we do run into them, you be careful."

"The ole Nineteenth can whip anybody," proclaimed Sam, "and the Iron Brigade can take on the whole rebel army."

"Maybe so," answered the lieutenant, "but even so, it's best to be careful."

"Oh, we will," said Ben. "My Momma would be angry with me if I hurt myself." With that, Lieutenant East laughed and walked away from his ex-students.

...e Morning's Fight

Annie Taylor was surprised when she heard the sounds of gunfire. The thirteen year old was in the stable, feeding her horse, Nutmeg, as the distant noise began to heighten. Nutmeg shook her huge brown head and whinnied, upset by the warlike sound. Annie gently patted the mare's neck, and softly whispered to her, and the Morgan relaxed, and then put her muzzle back down into the feed sack.

"What's that?" asked Annie's cousin, and close friend, Rachel Kendall.

Annie patted Nutmeg one more time and then walked to the stable window. The young teenager looked towards the west. Annie considered the rumbling noise and wondered. The sounds were much like what was heard when a thunderstorm was approaching. Annie frowned because these sounds were much more ominous. "Someone's shooting."

Rachel glanced at her younger cousin. Though there was exactly 11 months difference between the two girls, they were nearly the same height and build. If it were not for the fact that Annie had red hair while Rachel possessed black, there would have been almost no way to tell the two girls apart. People were always mistaking them for sisters.

"Do you think it's hunters?"

14

Rachel Kendall

Julia Evans Collection

Annie Taylor

Sandra Williams Collection

"If it's hunters, then every man in Adams County with a musket must be out after deer this morning. Rachel, there's way too much shooting for it to be hunters," answered Annie. She ran her slender hands through her auburn hair and gazed into the haze. As she studied the distant hills, she played absentmindedly with the gold pin attached to her collar.

"Oh, so it's all those soldiers we saw yesterday." Rachel smiled, thinking back to last evening, when hundreds of dust-covered horse soldiers had ridden along the Chambersburg Pike, and past the Taylor's house.

Annie's father, John Taylor, taught at the Lutheran Seminary and owned a large two-story brick home just beyond the seminary's grounds. Here, Annie had grown up, and for as long as the two cousins could remember, they had enjoyed running about the institution. Lately though, now that they were older, the two enjoyed spying on the dozens of handsome young men who would sit under the trees and study their books.

But yesterday had been different, and very special. Rachel and Annie had ridden Nutmeg into Gettysburg to take some things to Rachel's mom, Francis Kendall. When the two arrived, they found the townspeople buzzing with rumors. There was supposed to be a rebel army marching towards Gettysburg and no Yankee troops to stop them. Some people were leaving, having packed their valuables into buggies, hoping to escape by setting out for Harrisburg, or Baltimore. One fleeing family warned Annie and Rachel to get away before it was too late. The frightened woman told the cousins that rebels were devils who would steal them blind. The two teens had laughed at the woman as she and her family scurried away, their overloaded buggy's axles squealing.

However, as the girls were returning to Annie's house, slowly riding Nutmeg along Chambersburg Pike, a thunderous noise arose behind them. Turning to look, the cousins saw a long column of blue-coated soldiers galloping towards them. Annie immediately directed Nutmeg off the pike and the two watched the horsemen approach. As the column rushed towards them, the riders paired off into twos, with their lines stretching back as far as the girls could see. Then, the first of the horsemen were past them, the dust-covered cavalrymen intent on some distant objective down the road. More soldiers passed, and as other riders went by, Rachel and Annie began to wave at the dusty troopers. Most of the men ignored the two, but some smiled and waved back, and a few of the young men even called out to the girls, their hurried salutations making the cousins giggle.

"Yes, I think it's those soldiers," said Annie. She left the window and returned to her mare. But, as Annie rubbed Nutmeg's neck, she again found herself looking towards the sounds of combat.

Rachel reached out and grasped Annie's arm, her dark brown eyes bright with excitement. "Let's find a place where we can see what's happening." Rachel, since she was the older of the two, was often the one to suggest new adventures. Now, Rachel was fascinated by the idea of gazing at all of those good-looking Yankee troopers they had seen yesterday.

"Father will be furious." Annie frowned as she considered Rachel's idea. The younger cousin often was the more cautious of the two girls, though she was usually open to Rachel's adventures. Annie rubbed her beloved horse's neck and closed her green eyes. Their parents knew that the two liked to investigate their world, and though neither were prone to get themselves into serious trouble, they often found themselves in hot water.

"Yes, he will. If he finds out." She smiled innocently at her cousin. "Annie Taylor, this is a once-in-a-lifetime chance to see a battle. If we don't do it now, we'll never get another chance. What will you tell your grandchildren when they ask you if you saw the war?"

Annie thought for a moment, stroking Nutmeg gently. Outside, off to the west, the girls could hear the tempo of the fight increasing as the scattered shots from individual rifles grew into a continuous angry rumble.

"We could climb to the top of the seminary," suggested Rachel, her eyes flashing. Annie still clung to Nutmeg. "Oh, come on, Annie, we won't get in trouble." Rachel pulled at her cousin's arm and dragged Annie out of the stable.

Once they were outside Annie's hesitation quickly evaporated. Once she made up her mind, she often was more aggressive than her older relative. Annie, her red hair flying in the breeze, led the way towards the stately seminary buildings. The roar of the distant fight was louder than before. Suddenly several thundering crashes boomed out, making the girls jump.

"Those are cannons," proclaimed Rachel. "Come on, we've got to hurry." With that, both girls began to race for the Lutheran Seminary.

The Lutheran Seminary's main building was a huge brick structure, being one hundred feet long and forty feet wide. The main building, as it was called, had been built in 1832 and was the most prominent structure west of Gettysburg. It was the heart of the seminary, with its classrooms and book-filled library. The building was also home to the Ziegler family, including their friend, Lydia.

Rachel and Annie expected to find Lydia reading a book, sitting at the top of the steps, as she so loved to do, but soon discovered she was absent and the massive wooden doors were securely locked. But the cousins knew of a side entrance into the seminary and quickly found their way into the empty building.

Inside, the air was dark and cool, and smelled of candles. Annie knew the way to the top floor, and from there to the ladder which took them up to the structure's cupola.

Once the girls were standing among the white-painted columns of the cupola they were astonished at what they could see. The summer morning's air was choked with smoke and haze. Off to the northwest of Chambersburg Pike a long line of bubbling, grayish-white clouds arose, almost obscuring the movements of the distant figures. Riders raced about, their horses kicking up dust wherever they went. As the girls watched, they could see little flashes of flame erupt from within that confusing mist. The twinkling of light reminded the girls of a multitude of fireflies flitting about.

A breath of air pushed the smoke aside and the girls recognized dark figures hunched down behind the zig-zag lines of a split rail fence. The soldiers were shooting their rifles, aiming at a far-off tree line. The cousins could also see a row of cannons, the gunners frantically hustling about the weapons. Then the guns vanished within huge clouds of white smoke. The booms from those guns took many seconds to reach the cousins. They hugged each other in excitement. For the next fifteen minutes the two watched spell-bound from their perch, pointing out battle flags, movements of men, and the effects of artillery explosions.

The girls also began to see a small number of men drifting back from the battle. Some of these fellows limped away from the firing lines by themselves, others staggered away in little groups as the soldiers helped each other, and in some cases, it was obvious that their comrades were carrying some of the troopers. Though the distance was great, Annie, who had extremely keen vision, was able to see that some of those men were wearing bandages. "Those boys have been hurt," she murmured sadly.

"Oh, dear," whispered Rachel sadly, as she clutched at one of the cupola's massive columns, "those poor boys."

"What are you doing up here?" a harsh voice challenged loudly. Annie and Rachel turned around in fright, shocked to find five blue-coated soldiers having crowded up into the cupola with them.

Rachel glanced at all five soldiers, looking briefly at the two older men, and then studying the two younger ones. The other man, a smaller version of the other four, smiled at the girls and said quietly, "Now Wes, it appears these two young ladies have found the best place to observe the day's action." The mustached officer took off his leather gloves and smiled at the girls. "I'm General John Buford. Those are my boys out there." He then shook hands with both girls, who gawked at him in awe, their cheeks blushing to a bright red.

"You're the general of the horse soldiers who came by here yesterday?" stammered Rachel. She inspected the officer who stood before her. He had a droopy mustache that was tinted with gray. His creased face was sunburned a deep brown. Buford smelled of horses, sweat, and leather. Yet, his appearance pleased her greatly. Rachel gave him a friendly smile.

Buford chuckled and eased his way to the cupola railing. "Yes, and my boys out there are going to give the rebels a thrashing." The officer motioned to his adjutants and they gently moved Annie and Rachel away from the railing. "Now ladies, it has been a real pleasure meeting you, but I've got to go to work. I'll have to ask you to leave now. Please go home and stay there until this action is over."

Rachel and Annie retreated down the ladder, their hearts pounding. The two did not say anything until they were outside of the seminary building. Then, while standing in the lane in front of the building, they looked up and saw the soldiers in the cupola. General Buford was studying the battlefield with a pair of field glasses and saying something to a man standing next to him. The soldier was writing down what the general was telling him. Rachel waved and one of the blue-coats raised his hand in salute to her.

"Oh," Rachel lamented, "it's always the men who get to do the exciting and important things." She turned to Annie, "I wish we could do something brave." Just then an artillery shell burst about one hundred yards away, the explosion earsplitting, and frightening. The two young teens screamed in terror, and then scampered back to the Taylor's house.

Once inside the comfortable brick house, Annie found a note from her mother, stating that she had gone into Gettysburg. Thus, the girls were all alone. But the sounds of fighting were so alluring, the cousins just had to watch. At first the girls were content to watch from an attic window but they could not see everything, so Annie and Rachel soon found themselves outside again.

Chapter 3

A Drink of Lemonade

The 19th Indiana had been given orders to close ranks and hurry up. The soldiers marched in four columns, speeding up the pace, hustling towards Gettysburg. Word flashed down the line, describing the fighting west of Gettysburg. The Union army's cavalry was struggling with rebel infantry and was slowly being pushed backwards. The generals needed the Iron Brigade to come in and save the day.

Ben was sweating now, struggling beneath the extra weight he was carrying. He was not so sure it had been a good idea to worry about that silly dream. Next to him, Johnny marched easily, his shoulders straight and his head up, watching the rising smoke billow up above the distant trees.

"It's going to be a hot one, today," he proclaimed.

"Uh-huh," was all Ben could answer, as he wiped at the sweat dripping down his face. All he did was smear the dust coating his damp skin.

A messenger galloped by, the horseman's mount covered with lathered sweat. "What's going on?" one of the Hoosiers hollered out.

"Bobby Lee's boys are up ahead," called the rider as he passed on by.

"Close up, close up!" shouted a 19th Indiana officer, "I want no straggling." The troops hustled northwards, hurrying towards Gettysburg, and to the sounds of the growing fight.

It seemed that with each step Ben took the roar of the battle increased. His experienced ears could now identify the sharp sounds of infantry muskets, as well as the higher pitched reports from cavalry carbines. He could also detect the differences between Parrot rifles and Napoleons, whenever those cannons were fired. His heart was pounding, both from his accelerated marching pace, as well as the anticipation of having to go into battle.

"There'll be the devil to pay!" shouted Sam as he lumbered along the gravel road, next to Ben.

"Close up, close up," called out an officer angrily, as he urged the boys forward. The regiment thundered northwards, every step taking the men closer to Gettysburg, and to the forthcoming conflict.

The head of the column reached the top of a small hill and then descended into a shallow hollow. When Ben's file came to the hilltop he was able to see for several miles in all directions. In front of him he could see a lengthy, dark blue line, snaking northwards. Ben knew this column was composed of soldiers, just like himself, with each man beginning to contemplate the dangers that lay ahead. Behind him, as far as he could see, was a long column of soldiers. It was the rest of the Union I Corps, nearly ten thousand men in all. The youth's heart filled with pride. The generals said that their corps was the best in the entire Union army, and that their brigade was the best in the corps.

"This sure beats being at home and working for your pa," said Sam, excitedly. Ben nodded, struggling under the weight of his pack. Before the war both Ben and Sam had worked for Ben's father, who owned a successful blacksmith's shop on the outskirts of their little Indiana town, called Selma. Sam had lived with the Ellis family, taking most of his pay in room and board. The two friends had worked well together, with Ben supplying the brains and Sam the brawn.

An errant artillery shell exploded not far from the blue column, causing the men to briefly hunch down. A small white cloud of smoke was soon all that remained, and it dissipated quickly as the troops hurried by.

A few minutes later the column halted and the soldiers had a chance to catch their breath. When he looked about he saw a red-bricked house next to the road. There were other farms buildings about, all neatly maintained, as were all of the farms in this area.

"Heavy, huh?" taunted his friend, good-naturedly.

"Yeah," groaned Ben, "I didn't think it would weigh so much."

"You want me to take my half?"

"No!"

"Well, okay, but tomorrow it'll be my turn to carry everything."

"Yep."

"Now listen up," called out Captain Orr. The men in Company K focused on their commander as he took off his large black hat and wiped at his short red hair. "The general wants us to remove our packs and stack them over there, next to that corncrib. There'll be a detail to guard our packs, so don't worry about your stuff." He paused for a few seconds, before pointing towards the sounds of battle. "There's supposed to be a division of rebs just west of Gettysburg. Our cavalry boys are holding them off, but we all know how good our cav' is. It's going to be up to us to kick the Johnnies back to Virginia. I hope you boys are ready for a fight!"

Some of the soldiers in Company K howled in response to their leader's words. "Lieutenant East, see to it that the boys' packs are stacked properly. I'll be back in a few moments."

"Yes, Captain," answered the assistant company commander. He turned to the company. "Quickly now, stack arms, break ranks, remove your packs, and then fall back in." A sergeant showed them where to pile the bedrolls and knapsacks, and then the men strolled back to the formation.

The men in Company K complied with Lieutenant East's orders and within just a couple minutes had completed their task. Ben was glad to be rid of the heavy pack, and felt ashamed for having worried about their gear. He wondered if his dream was nothing other than a veteran soldier's nightmare. Ben knew that many of his comrades had woken up in the dark of night, plagued by disturbing dreams. But Lieutenant East was getting the company reformed and Ben did not have anymore time to ponder his dreams.

The regiment was ordered to march again, but now they left the dust of Emmitsburg Road and headed west across a pasture of knee-high grass. The boys stumbled across the uneven field, trying to maintain their balance among the tall weeds that prevented them from being able to see the holes in the ground. Someone cried out in pain and fell out of formation, having sprained his ankle.

The roar of battle increased as the regiment left the pasture and thumped their way through a wooded lot. The rattle of musketry was sharp and distinct, as were the crashes of artillery. Occasionally, the boys could hear bugles. The three looked at each other, their faces now beginning to turn pale, because they had been in battles before and knew about war's terrors.

The column halted by several large stone brick buildings. Someone said the place was a Lutheran seminary. The three had traveled hundreds of miles during the past two years, and almost all of these journeys had been done on foot. There was little about where they went that interested them anymore. The boys' world was usually one of heat, sweat, and sore, blistered feet.

The resting soldiers stood about, watching other Federals hurry, first one way, and then in the other direction. The crash and booms of artillery thundered across the shady lawn where the regiment had stopped. The musketry was now continuous, causing the men to unconsciously tighten the muscles in their shoulders. Riders galloped about, and ammunition wagons rumbled past. Ambulances came and went, some loaded with moaning passengers, and others empty of occupants.

"Look, look," called out Sam. He was leaning against his rifle, scanning the sight before them. Sam pointed with a dirty hand towards two attractive girls who watched them. The shorter of the two had curly red hair that sparkled in the sunlight. The other's hair was dark and shiny. The two girls looked so similar that Sam whispered, "I bet they're sisters."

Sam waved to the girls, and flashed them his best smile. Ben and Johnny glanced at them covertly. They knew that Sam was the best there was for finding unattended animals or apple trees. He was also very good at noticing, and getting the attention of the local young ladies.

"Let's go meet them," he suggested, quickly looking around for the company's sergeants.

"We better stay in line," countered Johnny, who feared nothing, except girls. "The colonel may order us to move at any moment. We don't want to be left behind."

"When did you start worrying about being left behind?" asked Sam. "I just think you're yellow."

Johnny could not take being thought of as afraid so he gritted his teeth and hissed, "No I'm not." Johnny glanced about, noticing where the sergeants were, and saw them clustered together, talking.

"Follow me," Sam commanded, and slipped out of the ranks, quickly trailed by his shy friends. The two girls saw the boys approaching and chattered happily between themselves.

"Have you come to save us?" taunted Rachel, her smile easing the verbal harassment she tossed at the soldiers. She studied them as they approached. All three boys wore scuffed leather brogans, dirty, light blue pants, dark blue coats, each with a long row of shiny brass buttons, and huge dust-covered, black hats.

"Why yes we have," countered Sam bravely. He stopped a few feet away from the two cousins and bowed deeply. "Let me introduce myself, and my two trustworthy companions." The overtures were quickly made and then the five stood silently, rather embarrassed by their boldness. Ben noticed how nice the two girls smelled. He savored a light fragrance of soap and honeysuckle perfume. Ben wondered about his own odor. He imagined that he reeked mighty badly, as all soldiers did.

Then Annie spoke. Her young woman's voice was gentle to Ben's ears, "Are you boys thirsty? We have been passing out lemonade." She held up the ceramic pitcher, its crockery glistening with condensation. "There's not much left, but you can have it, if you'd like."

"Why, thank you, ma'am," said Ben, who had suffered all morning from the heat, and from the heavy pack he had been lugging.

"Give me your cup," Annie commanded. All three boys reached down to their haversacks and untied their army-issue tin cups. The boys crowded close to the two girls and Annie poured a couple ounces of lemonade into each rusted tin cup. The boys thanked her immensely, and sipped at the sweet liquid, trying to make those few drops last as long as possible.

"Do you live around here?" asked Sam, gazing with his faded brown eyes at Rachel's blushing face.

"I live in town," she answered, flashing the boys a big smile as she studied the three young soldiers. Their faces were dirty, as were their hands and fingernails. The boys smelled of sweat and leather. She wrinkled her nose at their odor.

"I live right over there," announced Annie, pointing with her delicate hand towards the Taylor house, hardly more than two hundred yards away. "Oh, this is so exciting!"

The gravely voice of Lieutenant East ruined the little group's joyous banter. He joined the five and said softly, "Boys, you'd better get back into line."

The young soldiers turned towards their officer, unhappily, their shoulders slumping in sadness. But they quickly said their good-byes, shook hands with Annie and Rachel, and unhappily returned to the company's ranks. The boys glanced back several times, and flashed little waves at the grinning cousins.

"I must warn you to be careful," cautioned the lieutenant, "the battle might come in this direction. I wouldn't want you to be caught out in it."

"Oh, you sound like my teacher," said Rachel.

The lieutenant chuckled. "Well, I was a teacher," he answered, "before the war. Those boys were some of my students." East glanced off into the distance and smiled dreamily. "Yeah, before the war."

"Where are you from?" asked Rachel, sensing the young lieutenant's homesickness.

"Selma," he replied, "Selma, Indiana. You've probably never heard of it. Selma is a little town not far from Muncie."

"Muncie?"

"Oh, you've never heard of Muncie, either."

"No. I wasn't much good in geography," admitted Rachel. She gave the handsome sunburned soldier another smile. Rachel guessed he might be 20, maybe 22. His accent was intriguing. It was much like the boys they had given the lemonade to, but she had not had enough time to listen to their words. Rachel bit at her lower lip, she figured that she never would get to hear them again, she thought sadly.

"Well," said Lieutenant East, "Muncie is probably 60 miles from Cincinnati. You have heard of Cincinnati?"

"Oh, yes," laughed Annie, "it's called the Queen City of the West. My mom likes to buy soap made by some company from there."

"Procter and Gamble?"

"Maybe. I think so."

Lieutenant East chuckled, and was going to say more but a sergeant hollered at him. The officer turned just in time to see the soldiers shoulder their muskets and move into a column.

"I've got to go. Now promise me this, ladies, you will go home and stay inside. We're going to be fighting nearby. It could get quite dangerous around here. I wouldn't want you to get hurt."

The cousins nodded, and then he unsheathed his long sword, saluted them, turned, and jogged back to the company. Both girls sighed.

"Indiana," said Annie, dreamily, "that's so far away. Those boys have come here from so far away. Oh, I would be so lonesome."

"But aren't they so handsome!" commented Rachel, still watching the boys as they marched around the end of the seminary buildings. Sam turned one more time and waved his huge black hat at them. Rachel waved back to him, and then impetuously, blew him a kiss.

"Rachel!" barked Annie. Then the two hugged each other and giggled.

Chapter 4

Ready for the Fight

Ben stood with Johnny on his left, Sam behind him, and a corporal to his right. The regiment had marched past the seminary and ascended a little ridge. The 19th Indiana was halted, and then maneuvered from a column of troops in marching formation into a long, thin battle line. Colonel Williams stood out in front of the regiment, examining his men. The Indiana veterans welcomed his inspection, liking their leader immensely, and willing to follow him anywhere.

Colonel Williams was a huge man, and was known for his intelligence, fairness, and for his hearty laugh. He had been the 19th's leader for just over six months, and during that short span of time had won everyone's respect. Before being promoted to colonel, Sam Williams, who was also from Selma, had been Company K's captain.

The colonel walked before his regiment, starting at the left and slowly working his way along the line. When he came to Company K he stopped and faced his old comrades. "Oh, my beloved boys," he whispered loudly. The Selma soldiers straightened their backs a little more and grinned.

Then Colonel Williams saw Ben and rapidly stepped up to him. "And how's my Benjamin Ellis, this hot morning?"

"Fine, sir," Ben replied sternly. Williams smiled and patted the young soldier on his shoulder. Ben beamed with pride.

"You take care of yourself today. There's danger over in those trees, yonder. You watch after yourself. Don't make me have to worry about you, do you hear?"

"Yes, sir. I will take care of myself, don't you worry."

Williams leaned back and roared in laughter, a healthy sound, causing all the soldiers around him to join in.

"No, son, I will do my best not to worry." Williams patted Ben on the shoulder a second time and then made his way along the line, slowly reviewing his troops. The men cheerfully responded to their beloved commander.

Ben flushed with pride. Colonel Williams had taken a moment at this busy time to recognize his young neighbor. The boy closed his eyes and thought back to before the war. The Ellis property had been right next to the Williams' estate. Sam Williams was a very successful farmer and had invested much of his profits in important livestock. Williams raised and sold valuable cattle and expensive sheep.

Ben had often been to the Williams farm, usually to help his father prepare horseshoes for Williams' horses. The other reason Ben liked to linger about the Williams farm was because of Rebecca, a lively, beanpole of a girl with a feisty disposition and a witty tongue. Rebecca Williams was a tomboy who could outrun and outwrestle most of the fellows, but when she put on her finery and showed up at a barn dance, she was as pretty a sight as a young lad could ever see. And, she always chose Ben whenever the girls got to pick a dancing partner!

Ben smiled, thinking back to those pleasant summer evenings when the Delaware County fair was being held. The days were usually hot and sultry but the youngsters did not mind. They would gather together, play baseball on the village commons, drink cold lemonade, eat ice cream, and buy penny fire-crackers. Then, once the sun had set, the musicians would tune up their instruments, people would bring lanterns to the barn, and everyone would dance un-til they were dripping wet from sweat.

When the war broke out in April 1861, Sam Will-iams decided to raise a militia company of infantry. Williams got Selma's flourishing young lawyer, William Orr, to help him, and the two began recruiting volun-teers from among their neighbors and friends. The local response to the call for volunteers was tremen-dous, and soon their militia company was known as the Selma Legion. Ben was in a frenzy to enlist but he was not quite 14. His parents refused to even con-sider his pleadings, saying he was too young.

A month later, when the village of Selma proved to be too small to provide Williams and Orr with the required hundred men to complete their company, Indiana state officials informed them that they could not come to Indianapolis to be mustered into the army. When Indiana's first five regiments were sent off to the war, Williams and Orr could only watch the lucky volunteers leave. Therefore, in an effort to get the last volunteers to enter their formation's ranks, the two Selma men lowered their age standards. Selma Legion recruiters were allowed to sign excited teen-agers who were younger than the required 18 years of age.

Johnny and Sam, both big kids for their young age of 14, quickly finagled their way onto the Selma Legion's rolls. Ben became frantic as he watched his friends drill on the Selma school yard, marching to the right and left to the commands of Crockett East, their teacher-turned-drill sergeant. Ben fumed in frustration, it was just not fair that Sam and Johnny could go off to war and become heroes, and he had to stay home simply because he had been born a couple months later.

Sam Williams saw the longing in Ben's eyes, and still needed a couple more names to complete the Selma Legion's roll sheets. He conspired with the young blacksmith to wrangle a way to get Ben on the company's muster roll. Sam came to Ben's parents and admitted the boy was too young to be a rifleman. However, Sam argued, the company also needed drummers, and Ben was the right age to be a musician. Plus, Sam promised that he personally would insure that Ben was kept out of danger. Ben's parents reluctantly agreed and granted their ecstatic son permission to join Sam Williams' company.

Not long after Ben had been issued his coveted gray-and-red militia uniform, the Selma Legion was ordered to Indianapolis. There, Captain Williams' boys trained with thousands of other Hoosiers, sweating horribly in the muggy summer's heat. Finally, in late July 1861 the Selma Legion was mustered into the 19th Indiana regiment, to be designated as Company K, and to be under the command of Colonel Solomon Meredith.

"Long Sol," as the boys called their colonel, was a huge man, towering over everyone, standing six-foot-seven. Meredith soon loaded his regiment onto train cars, bound for Washington City, including the excited Private Benjamin Ellis, who Captain Williams rapidly discovered could not keep even the simplest drumbeat, but was as good as the next Hoosier at shooting a musket, and filling a slot in the ranks. As the thousand exhilarated farm boys and shopkeepers making up Meredith's regiment joyously rolled out of Indianapolis, the elated volunteers were impatient to meet rebels, defeat them, and come home, heroes.

Now, two years later, barely three hundred Hoosiers were still surviving to answer at the 19th Indiana's roll calls. Ben had become a veteran soldier during those two long years. He had been in several horrible battles: Gainesville, Second Bull Run, South Mountain, Antietam, Fredericksburg, and Fitzhugh's Crossing. Ben knew a lot about war, having seen his neighbors hurt and killed. He had also helped bury friends who had died of sickness.

Ben had marched hundreds of miles under rainy skies, or in blistering heat, just to be ordered to turn around and march back to where the regiment had been before. He had lain out shivering on frozen fields with only a thin wool coat to protect him from the cold. Ben had endured endless days of rain, and roads filled with seemingly bottomless pits of mud. The boy-soldier had gone hungry, eaten spoiled and rotten foods, and suffered from drinking tainted water.

And yet Ben and his two close friends, Sam and Johnny, had survived everything. Oh, they had gotten the sickness, in Washington City, along with everyone else. But they had not died, no, they recovered and marched with the regiment wherever it had been ordered to go. The three had stood, shoulder to shoulder, in the regiment's battles and had come out of each terrifying action frightened, but miraculously unscathed. Now, here on July 1, 1863, just west of the small town of Gettysburg, Pennsylvania, the boys' regiment was preparing to go back into battle.

Chapter 5

Danger at the Seminary

Annie and Rachel did not take the handsome lieutenant's advice and retreat to the safety of the Taylor household. Instead, the two cousins drifted over to a small crowd forming in front of the Lutheran Seminary's main building. There were two well-used ambulances now parked by the steps. The vehicles' horses were tired and covered with lather. Soldiers were unloading wounded men from the vehicles and carrying them inside the large building. The two girls could not resist the temptation to get closer and see what was happening.

When Annie pushed her way past the seminary students, who stood gawking, she was disappointed to find that both carriages were empty. Annie, who loved animals with a passion, rapidly inspected the horses and discovered they were exhausted. She felt pity for the weary beasts, and then was glad that Nutmeg was safely in her stall.

"Look," cried Rachel, her voice shrill. She pointed to some glistening stains upon the main building's stone steps. "I think that's blood."

"Blood?" A feeling of revulsion swept through Annie. She hated to see any animals hurt, and had been known to rescue birds with broken wings and care for

36

lost puppies. Now, she could see bright splashes of blood spilled upon the steps, almost as if someone had been carelessly carrying a pail of red paint and had allowed some paint to drip.

Suddenly Rachel heard a moan. It was a horrible sound, that of a man suffering intense pain. She shuddered and stepped back, her face turning pale. An alarming realization came to her. Soldiers who had been shot now occupied the seminary, the same building where she and Annie had once played. That vivid red which was splattered against the white stones of the building's steps had not been sloshed from a can of paint, but rather had dripped from some poor boy whose body had been punctured and torn by a musket ball.

"Let's go," Rachel whispered hoarsely, backing away even as she said the words. Annie, her eyes wide with horror, took her hand and the two cousins hurried away. A scream came from the seminary, the shrill noise coming out of an opened window. The girls grabbed their long, hoop skirts, lifted them up, and then ran.

As Annie and Rachel sprinted towards the Taylor house they realized the war had come to them. There were now hundreds of soldiers everywhere. The hot, dust-covered troops hurried about, some in long columns, others in little clusters, and a few just individually. Riders galloped past, their mounts kicking up dust and clods of dirt. The sounds of rifle fire were close by, and all too often, the girls heard the angry buzz of a passing bullet. The cousins ran as fast as they could, dodging in and out of the lines of sweaty soldiers.

Soldiers yelled at the girls, some calling to them, others shouting for them to get out of the way. Annie and Rachel thought they were never going to make it back home. They had to detour around six cannons of a Federal artillery battery setting up barely a hundred

yards from the Taylor house. The cannoneers were
bustling around the large weapons, using slender poles
to push ammunition into the long, black gun tubes.

When the two girls finally reached the safety of
the brick Taylor house they were dismayed to find a
handful of soldiers lounging on their porch chairs.
Rachel and Annie, though still out of breath, gathered together their courage and approached the
porch.

"What are you doing here?" demanded Rachel,
straightening herself up as tall as she could. She directed her question to a tired soldier with stripes on
his shoulder.

The man glared at her, his weary eyes dull from
fatigue. Then, when he saw how frightened Rachel was,
his face softened and he smiled at her. "Don't fret,
lassie. I be Sergeant Patrick Collins. I'll be of no harm
to yah." He stared at her for a moment and then stood
up. "Where are me manners, I ask me-self. Here stands
two young lassies and I be on their front porch. What
an eejit I am. Me lads and I, we were just resting on
your front porch."

"This is my home; you don't belong here," asserted
Annie, stepping up onto the wooden porch. Annie's
face was bright red and her small hands were balled
into tight fists.

"And your pa, tell me where he would be," countered the Irish sergeant.

"He's at the seminary, right over there," Annie
answered pointing over her shoulder. "He'll be here
very soon. You'd better go away before he gets here,
or else he'll be very angry."

"And will he now, come home right away, just as
the sweet little lassie, here is a say'un," said the sergeant with a laugh.

"Yes Pa will," stammered Annie. She glared at the
big man angrily. "Now, I want you to go!" The sergeant

looked down at the small girl, chewed on something in his mouth for a few seconds, and then began to grin.

"Do you now? Holy saints preserve us. And you being such a wee little thing. I ask me-self, does Patrick Collins want this colleen to think him ah amazon?"

"If we give you something to eat and drink, then will you go away?" asked Rachel, also stepping up on the porch. She stepped lightly around the big sergeant and looked at the other soldiers who were loafing on the porch. They had been following the spirited exchange between Sergeant Collins and Annie, their dust-caked faces amused by her spunk.

"Sergeant," one of the soldiers called out, "it sounds like these two little ladies are getting the best of you. I think we ought to take their offer of eats, and then get going on our way. You know the captain will soon be noticing our absence."

"Do you now? And you be wearing me sergeant stripes so soon." Collins turned to the girls, who struggled to keep from quivering. "And isn't this wee lassie as brave as any man in County Galway?" He leaned back, a twinkle in his eyes, and roared in laughter. "Aye, me little colleen. Some fix'uns it will be. Then, we'd better be off, hadn't we now." He stepped back to let the two pass. Their hearts pounding, they rushed past the sergeant and scurried into the house, making sure to lock the door, once inside.

Standing in the hallway, Annie and Rachel hugged each other, both trembling from fear. "What do we do now?" asked Annie, her knees still shaking.

"Let's feed them. Then let's get out of here."

"Yes. We'll ride Nutmeg and go to your home. I want to get away from this horrible war."

After counting how many soldiers lingered on the porch, the two cousins took a loaf of bread and sliced it into thick pieces. Then they cut up some tomatoes, and piled bread, scraps of ham and slices of cheese onto the bread. There was no more lemonade, so they just got a pitcher of water.

Gathering together their courage, the cousins opened the door and passed the sandwiches out to the hungry men. Each soldier gently took the food into his dirty hands and then thanked them profusely. And, to their great relief, the little squad of soldiers took up their rifles and sauntered off, heading towards the furious sounds of battle.

Just as soon as the men were off the front porch Annie rushed up to her room and packed a carpet bag with things she would need to spend the night at her cousin's house. Her father had not yet returned, but the girls did not want to wait any longer. Even as they gathered Annie's clothes the roar of battle increased in intensity.

Annie left a note on the kitchen table, explaining that she had gone to Gettysburg to be with Rachel. The two then slipped out of the house and ran down to the stable. Nutmeg was frightened and stomped around in her stall. It took Annie several minutes to calm the anxious Morgan. Then she put a bridle on the mare and led the nervous horse out of the stall.

Nutmeg flinched when the nearby cannons erupted in thunder and danced around in a circle, jerking Annie off her feet. The young teen hung onto the reins and soothed the terrified animal. The battle was raging everywhere now, and there seemed no way to go to get away, except straight back to Gettysburg. Finally, Annie calmed Nutmeg enough to allow the girls to climb onto her back. Annie, who could ride as good as any Adams County boy, firmly guided the spooked mare onto a path leading to the Chambersburg Pike.

"Look," said Rachel, pointing back to the Taylor house. When Annie turned around and glanced at her home she saw an ambulance pulling up and parking by their porch. Union soldiers quickly climbed out.

Within seconds the blue-uniformed troops began unloading wounded men and carrying them up onto the
porch. The Yanks were going to use her house for a
hospital.

"Oh, Mother will be furious if they break anything,"
cried Annie. An artillery shell blew up not far from the
girls, spewing mud and cornstalks in all directions. The
explosion startled Nutmeg and she began to run. Both
girls were accustomed to riding double-back, so when
the Morgan went into a gallop, they rode easily, quite
familiar with her smooth swaying motion.

The Chambersburg Pike was crowded with wagons, horses, and columns of troops. Once Nutmeg had
run the terror out of her system Annie was able to
keep her at a brisk trot. The girls also noticed that the
soldiers now marching along the pike had little white
half-moons on their hats. Annie and Rachel recalled
that the three soldier-boys they had met barely an
hour ago had little red circles on their hats.

When the girls reached the west end of Gettysburg
they saw many people looking out of upstairs windows and balconies, or just standing at their door-
steps. Others had climbed up onto the rooftop of the
Fahnestock Brother's Store. Everyone was looking towards the west, trying to figure out what was going
on. A few townspeople asked the girls where they had
been and what they had seen, but Annie and Rachel
did not stop to answer. The two wanted to get to the
Kendall home just as fast as Nutmeg could get them
there.

The girls went straight into town, working their
way eastwards on Chambersburg Street. When they
reached the center of town, at the wide intersection
called the Diamond, Annie turned Nutmeg southwards,
onto Baltimore Street. They now were only two blocks
from the Kendall house. Annie turned the mare to the
left onto East Middle Street, and then quickly to the

right, and into an alley. Here, they came to the Kendall's carriage house, dismounted, and stabled Nutmeg. Then the girls ran past the Kendall vegetable garden, and to Rachel's back door.

Both of the girls' mothers were there, and were glad to see their daughters. Rachel and Annie described what they had seen but did not mention the dangers they had encountered. Since the girls did not want to upset their mothers they told their story and made it sound like the battle was just a little skirmish.

Chapter 6

Into the Battle

Ben gazed out across the empty pasture that lay before their regiment, his hands quivering in fear. There were nearly four hundred yards of open ground to cover before reaching the distant line of trees. Ben shuddered. He guessed the rebels were lurking in those trees, just waiting for the 19th Indiana to get within range of their muskets.

"It's going to be the devil, crossing this field," said the corporal next to him.

Ben nodded. He reached over and touched Johnny's sleeve, drawing comfort from his friend's nearness. Standing behind the two boys, Sam reached forward and patted them on their shoulders.

"Come on, Colonel, let us at 'em," Sam growled.

Then, almost as if he had been waiting for permission, Colonel Williams gave the order for the regiment to advance. The 19th Indiana's large American flag was moved forward, carried by a stout sergeant. Another banner was carried next to the national colors. This standard was dark blue and contained a huge eagle stitched onto its center. The regiment's flags flapped in the warm morning air.

Colonel Williams marched out in front of the flags, held his sword in the air, and then shouted, "March!" With that, the entire regiment, nearly three hundred men, stepped forward. The formation moved forward quietly, as there were no drummers. The musicians had been left behind to guard the regiment's packs.

Johnny, who had excellent eyesight, noticed movements in the trees. His heart was pounding as he waited for the rebels to start shooting. Each measured step he took brought him closer to the Southerner's rifles. The young soldier hunched down, waiting for that first perilous volley.

Next to him, Ben also had tightened his shoulders' muscles, and leaned forward. The young soldier's brogans thudded softly on the pasture's grasses, in step with the men surrounding him. The 19th quickly covered 50 yards of the pasture, and yet, nothing had happened. But Ben had been in too many battles to let his hopes overrule the reality of the situation. The veteran knew the gray-coats had to be waiting for them and was just waiting for the right time to ambush his unprotected regiment. He just knew they would start shooting.

Sam clenched his teeth in fear. He knew that everyone thought him to be stone-hard courageous. But that was not really the case. The young man was just very good at bluffing, and making everyone think he was bold-hearted. Right now, he was terrified. Sam knew that he had been in six major battles, and a batch of little skirmishes, and had never been hurt. Wondering when his luck would run out, he ground his teeth in consternation, but yet kept in step with everyone else. He was determined to do his share, and not be called a coward by anyone.

The regiment slowed down its pace and almost stopped when it was about one hundred yards from the wood line. Everyone expected the rebels to open fire, but yet, nothing had happened. The sergeants and officers yelled encouragement to the anxious soldiers and the riflemen picked up their pace and hurried towards the trees.

Ben sighed in relief when the Hoosiers crashed into the underbrush. The regiment had crossed the open field without a mishap. Oh, what a mistake the rebels had made, letting them get across that pasture. Now, when the Indiana boys found the rebels and pitched into them, at least everyone could hide behind the trees.

The Yanks slowly worked through the woods, busting their way through the brambles and vines. The regiment's straight line had broken into small knots of men, as the troopers clustered around their leaders and friends. The underbrush was thick, preventing the men from seeing more than a few yards. However, the woods were alive with their noise. The men shouted to each other as they stomped through the vegetation.

Rifle fire erupted off to Ben's right, causing him to pause for a second. Then, his experience took over. Ellis knew that the shooting was far enough away that he was not in immediate danger. He peered into the trees ahead of him and searched for the rebels, while moving forward.

Suddenly, the Hoosiers came out of the trees and underbrush, and into in a clearing. A sluggish stream divided the clearing, the shallow water moving slowly over the tops of flat rocks. Captain Orr and Lieutenant East quickly lined up the company and squared them with the company on their right. Another company formed up on their left. This procedure only took the veterans a few moments.

Ben looked to his right and was surprised to see a thin line of rebels, maybe a hundred yards upstream. The Johnnies were busy firing at the other half of the Hoosier regiment. The experienced soldier quickly realized that the Southerners did not even know these three Indiana companies were approaching them.

The company commanders were veterans and immediately responded to this piece of good fortune.

Captain Orr called for a right wheel. This maneuver swung the three Hoosier companies around so that they would become much like the top half of the letter *T*, with the rebels' position being the lower portion. The Westerners would be able to fire down the entire length of the Confederate position without the gray-coats being able to effectively shoot back.

Sam hollered in triumph as they completed their wheel. It was seldom that a force was ever able to accomplish this flanking maneuver, but they had! He brought up his musket when their red-haired captain ordered Company K to prepare to shoot. Seconds later the weapon bucked against his shoulder when he fired.

The young soldier did not know if he had hit anybody with his shot, and he really did not want to know. However, now that his weapon had been discharged, the rifleman automatically began to reload the piece, a process he knew would take about 20 seconds. He had already bitten off the end of the paper cartridge and then dumped the black powder down the musket's barrel. Ben pushed the bullet down the weapon's barrel with the ramrod and then, placed a new primer cap on the weapon's nipple. The youth raised the loaded rifle to the "aim" position, sighted on the mass of rebels, and pulled the trigger. The Springfield thundered, spewing flame and smoke, and propelling a Minié bullet towards the Confederates.

Smoke billowed up from the company's battle line as the Hoosiers poured a concentrated fire into the surprised Southerners. A few gray-clad men pitched over backwards, while others just slumped to the ground, dropping like sacks of potatoes. Many more cowered away from the destructive Yank's musketry, and a handful threw down their weapons and began to run away.

But not all of the rebels were startled by the sudden onslaught of the Indiana soldiers. The Johnnies were also veterans of two years of war, just like the Hoosiers. These steady old hands knelt down, took aim at the blue-coats, and began to return fire.

A bullet zipped past Ben's head, buzzing like an angry bee. Another kicked up dirt at the youth's feet, but he gritted his teeth and finished reloading his rifle. Ben sent his next shot off as quickly as possible and then, once again, started the laborious procedure of recharging his weapon.

Johnny stood at Ben's left, loading and firing just as quickly as his friend. Neither boy said anything, though many of the other soldiers cursed and yelled as they fought. Both boys had learned many battles ago that shouting only made them hoarse, and worse—terribly thirsty for the precious water in their tin canteens.

A round musket ball, traveling at about nine hundred feet per second, slammed into Johnny's left brogan, exactly between the first and second bootlace. The heavy sphere of lead punched through the thin leather and tore through tissue and bone, and ripped the badly damaged foot almost completely from his leg. The injured boy fell forward, landing on his belly and face.

Even though Ben stood right next to his friend, he was so involved in loading and firing that he did not realize Johnny had gone down. He was like a machine, thoughtless and methodical, his arms and hands worked so efficiently he did not even have to think. He continued to shoot bullets into the rebel position.

The Confederate line finally broke. Captain Orr ordered the Hoosiers to charge. The soldiers leaped forward, howling fiercely at the cringing Southerners and surged across the remaining yards separating the two forces.

The beaten rebels threw down their muskets and jerked their hands into the air, pleading for the Hoosiers to stop shooting. The Hoosiers swarmed among the whipped Southerners and captured dozens.

Ben suddenly was face to face against a huge Southerner with a wild, mangy beard. The reb's eyes were wide with terror, and he held his dirty hands up in front of his face, crying for mercy.

"Kneel!" shouted Ben, his emotions at a high pitch. The rebel complied instantly, dropping to the ground. Ben hovered over the big man, and without thinking, roughly placed his musket on the reb's shoulder. The Southerner wailed in distress. Ben looked down and saw that his sizzling-hot rifle barrel had quickly burnt through the soldier's coat and shirt. The odor of broiling flesh assailed Ben's nose. He immediately removed the weapon from the man's shoulder.

"I'll take care of him," said the calming voice of Lieutenant East. Ben looked at the officer and had to blink his eyes several times before the battle haze lifted from his brain. The teenager glanced down at the prisoner, who cringed before him, and saw the blisters forming on the man's skin.

"I burned him," Ben said sadly.

"Oh, he'll be okay," replied Lieutenant East, "that'll knock the cockiness from his system." The officer looked around, and then back at Ben. "I want you to find the first sergeant and tell him to get the company together."

"Yes, sir." Ben lifted his weapon and worked his way through the disorganized maze of Yanks and captured rebs. Ben spotted the first sergeant and gave him the lieutenant's message. He nodded and promptly started hollering for his corporals and sergeants.

The chaos only lasted for a few more minutes before the squad leaders had gathered their riflemen together and rallied the company. The prisoners captured by Company K were handed over to other soldiers and then the company was reformed. At that time Ben noticed Johnny was missing from the ranks. He and Sam called for Lieutenant East and the officer made his way to their position.

"Johnny's missing," said Ben breathlessly.

"Yeah, I don't know where he is," added Sam.

"He's probably still lost in that mess over there," answered East, pointing to a disorganized crowd of soldiers and prisoners. However, the lieutenant called for one of his sergeants and sent him out to locate the missing youth. The Hoosiers had all learned from experience that whenever someone was missing it was important to quickly find that man, because no one knew when the unit would be moved again.

Indeed, the regiment was moved a few minutes later. Colonel Williams led the 19th Indiana forward, splashing across the little boulder-strewn river and advancing up the clay slopes on its western side. The Indianans watched as the last of the retreating Confederates vanished into the trees, about a half mile away. The Yanks were exuberant, they had flanked the rebels and destroyed them. A large number of rebs had been captured, and it was even rumored that a Confederate general had been caught. It had been so easy, and so painless.

When the men were ordered to stack their rifles and rest, Ben looked back where they had been fighting but could not see any sign of Johnny. Going to Lieutenant East, he asked, "Can Sam and I go look for him?"

"Yeah," added Sam, "it's not like Johnny to run off. We've been together for two years. He's always been first-rate dependable."

"I know you are worried about your friend," said Lieutenant East, who scanned the company to see if there were any problems, "but I've got Sergeant Daughterly out looking for him. He's a good man, he'll locate Baker and bring him back." The two boys relaxed.

Though they wanted to go themselves, the youths realized that 27-year-old Tom Daughterly was very reliable. Everyone in the company liked Tom and would do just about anything he told them to do. Lieutenant East understood the boys' fears for their friend but would not let them leave the area. The officers did not want his youngest troopers to be wandering around by themselves. Though the Iron Brigade had busted apart a Confederate force and driven them away, the experienced officer sensed that this fight was not over. The heavy sounds of shooting north of where the 19th Indiana rested hinted at a coming involvement for the Hoosiers. Lieutenant East shuddered as he listened to the lethal sounds of combat, maybe a mile away. He closed his eyes and wished he were back home in Selma.

Chapter 7

The Rebel Horsemen

Once Rachel and Annie were finished eating, Rachel's mother asked the two girls to go get Rachel's eight-year-old brother. Robert was visiting one of his friends. The girls jumped at the chance to go out again and quickly agreed to go and fetch Robert. Even though Rachel and Annie had been alarmed by what had taken place near the theological seminary, they were ready for another adventure. The two assured their mothers that there were no soldiers north of Gettysburg, and that they would be extremely careful.

Though neither girl would have much to do with Rachel's dumb little brother, he was the perfect excuse for them to get out of the house and view more of the excitement. Robert was visiting his friend, Billy Ross, who lived on a farm about a mile north of town. Going to get the youngster was all the excuse the girls needed to get out and see what was happening.

Annie got Nutmeg ready, a task much more difficult than normal because the mare was quite nervous about all of the gunfire. However, the girl soothed the spooky Morgan and the cousins climbed up on top of her. Instead of heading straight north on Baltimore Street, the two went west onto High Street. The girls had decided to go to their school, the Young Ladies' Seminary, and retrieve some of the flower bouquets they had been making. Annie and Rachel wanted to give the pretty bouquets to the arriving soldiers.

The Young Ladies' Seminary was on the corner of Washington and High, in the southwest part of town. As the girls headed towards their school they were surprised to find that the streets were crowded with Gettysburg's black citizens, all fleeing. Rachel recognized Luther, a woodchopper who supplied the Kendall's with their firewood. His wife and their three little children accompanied the muscular worker.

"Luther," she called out to the huge black man. He was leading an old mule, loaded down with their household goods. "Luther, where you going?"

"Oh, Miss Rachel," he answered nervously, "for de Lord's sake, you children turn back right now. If dem rebs catch you dey tear you all up!"

"Luther, there's nothing to worry about. Our boys will take care of everything."

"Maybe so—maybe not. But if de rebs catch us dey steal us away, back to Virginnee. Ain't no way dis poor free-boy gonna' be no slave."

"Luther, that won't happen."

"Dat's right 'cause Luther's tak'un his family ta Balt'more. An' you, Missy, you be mighty careful, dem rebs catch you, de take you away too!"

"Come, Luther," commanded his wife, "there ain't no time to linger." With that Luther lifted his dusty felt hat to Annie and Rachel, turned and tugged at his mule, and then led his family away, hurrying down the street, leaving the two girls to make their way through the crowd of fleeing blacks.

"Do you think the rebels would take the coloreds back to Virginia?" asked Annie, her freckled face frowning in concern.

"I hadn't thought about it." Rachel wiped at the perspiration beading on her forehead. "But we won't have to worry about it. Our boys are going to whip the rebels. You heard General Buford. He told us his soldiers were going to thrash them."

"Oh, I sure hope so. I wouldn't want Luther to be captured and taken back to the South to be a slave."

"Me, neither." The two girls slowly made their way along High Street, staring at the fearful blacks as they quietly made their way down the dusty avenue.

Annie and Rachel reached the Young Ladies' Seminary and Rachel jumped off Nutmeg. The quick-footed girl raced into the stately building. Once inside she hurried into the main classroom and saw the piles of paper-silk flower bouquets which all the girls had been making. Rachel gathered up a handful.

"And just what are you doing?" Rachel turned around slowly and saw the pinched face of Miss Sally Wagstaff, the seminary's assistant teacher. The heavyset woman, her fleshy cheeks flushed with heat and sweat, glared at Rachel. She then whined, "You're not here to steal our bouquets, are you?"

"Oh no," said Rachel quickly, inching backwards, holding the handful of wrapped artificial flowers close to her chest. "I was going to take some to give to the soldiers," she stammered.

"You will put them back, right this very instant!" commanded the angry teacher.

"Yes, Miss Wagstaff," said Rachel, who immediately set the flowers back down on the table. She glanced up at the huge woman, who stared down at her with a look of hatred.

"I will make a note of this, Miss Kendall, and will inform Mrs. Smithson when she gets in. "Your thievery will not go unpunished. I will see to that."

Angry at what had taken place, Rachel wanted to fight back. She knew that the assistant would tell the seminary's headmistress, and make Rachel's innocent actions sound like a serious crime. She had only wanted to give some of the flowers to the soldiers. But then, to Miss Wagstaff, anything the girls did was a horrible wrongdoing. Thus, in a flash of spitefulness, Rachel snatched up two bouquets and dashed out of the room.

"Where are you going with those?" screeched the spinster. "You come back here right now."

Rachel ran out of the building and rushed up to Annie. "Quick, let's get out of here." Hardly had she spoken when the school's front door was pushed open and Miss Wagstaff thundered out. She pointed at the girls and began to yell.

"Come on, Nutmeg, save us!" laughed Annie who urged her Morgan to take them to safety. The big horse carried them north on Washington Street, the two girls giggling at their close call with the seminary's mean witch.

The sounds of fighting came from the west as menacing thunder. The girls could hear the steady popping of muskets and the louder booms from the artillery. Rachel, who clung to her cousin, listened to the battle noises and shuddered. She had seen the violence up close, and actually heard bullets zip past their heads. Rachel stared towards the west but all that could be seen in the late morning's haze were clouds of dust and smoke.

Directing Nutmeg onto Chambersburg Street, they made their way back to the center of town. Once at the Diamond the girls headed north on Carlisle Street. The riders passed the railroad station and made their way out of Gettysburg, Annie being forced to keep a firm hand on Nutmeg, who pranced about, jittery from the shooting.

The street traffic ceased just as soon as the girls were outside of town. Nutmeg made her way along the dirt and gravel road, heading towards the Ross farm. The rumble of gunfire continued, its ugly sounds causing the girls to continually glance over their shoulders towards the west. But all that could be seen were dust clouds.

When the girls reached the Ross farm, Billy's mother, Sarah, rushed to them, her eyes wide with fear. "Oh, it's so dangerous for you to be out," she called, even before they could dismount from Nutmeg.

"Oh, Mrs. Ross, it's okay. It's so exciting! We've been everywhere, today."

"You have? Well, it certainly isn't proper for two young ladies to be out, all by themselves, with so much commotion going on. Why, who knows what kind of danger is lurking about. Your mother would be furious if she knew what you were doing?"

"Ma sent us here," said Rachel, angry that Mrs. Ross was treating her like a child. "She wants us to bring Robert home."

"Oh, she did, did she? Well, if I had a daughter your age I certainly wouldn't let her out on a day like this," Sarah sniped. "It just isn't proper."

"Mrs. Ross, we'd like to stay and chat but Ma wants us home just as quickly as can be," said Rachel, gritting her teeth in frustration.

"Yes, I would imagine that she does," said Sarah primly. "Well, Billy and Robert are up at the barn. Billy's still doing his chores. It's not good for young boys to not have responsibilities."

"Yes, Mrs. Ross," answered both girls, rolling their eyes at each other. "We'll just go up there and get Robert and then be on our way."

"Hmmph," snorted the worried woman. "You tell my Billy that he must hurry up with his chores and then get back to the house."

"Yes, Mrs. Ross." Annie led around behind the stone house and followed a well-worn path to the huge barn, not far away. The girls called for Robert when they got near but he did not answer. "It figures," fumed Rachel. She went inside the barn and found the two boys armed with sticks, playing at sword fighting.

Robert was not happy to have to go, especially since he would have to be traveling with his older sister, but her angry glare subdued the boy's thoughts of resistance. He bid Billy good-bye and followed after Rachel. Once Rachel was outside of the barn, she could, again, hear the rumble coming from the west.

"What's that?" asked Robert as the three moved south on Bendersville Road.

"It's the battle," said Rachel, feeling important to be able to tell her little know-it-all brother what was going on.

"You mean the Yankees and rebels are fighting?"

"Yes, dummy."

"Wow, let's go see," he said, gazing into the haze.

"No, Ma wants us to go straight home."

"Ah, just a little peek, I won't tell Ma."

"No!"

"Come on, Sis, it'll only take a minute or two."

"No."

"Why not?"

"I already told you."

"Well," said Robert defiantly, "since you're too yellow, I'll just go by myself." He stopped and glared up at Rachel, his hands on his hips, daring her to confront him.

"Robert," yelled Rachel, "you will not!"

"What, how you going to stop me?" The brother and sister stared at each other, their eyes blazing with anger. This was not the first time that Robert and Rachel had fought, nor would this be the last time.

"Wait," said Annie, but the two combatants continued at their brother-sister war. Then Annie shouted, "Wait a moment!"

"What?" asked Rachel, indignant that her war of wills with Robert was being interrupted.

"There's riders coming."

"So," said Rachel glaring at her sullen brother.

"Rachel, you've got to stop. This could be a problem." At that, Rachel broke eye contact with Robert and glanced up the road. A party of horsemen was galloping towards them. At first she thought the riders were more Union soldiers until she realized their uniforms were completely different.

A bolt of fear flashed through Rachel's system. Those were Confederates approaching, and if the girls and Robert did not start moving right now, the rebels would capture them.

"Those are rebels!" she shrieked. "We've got to get out of here."

Robert turned and saw the Southern horsemen and wailed, "Don't leave me, Sis." There was no hatred in his voice, just terror.

"Quick, get up on Nutmeg," ordered Annie. The two cousins reached down and pulled the tow-headed youngster up onto the fidgety horse. "Run, Nutmeg," shouted Annie, "go with the wind."

Nutmeg, burdened by the three youths, took to a gallop, finally getting to release her pent-up fear. The large animal pounded southwards, down the road, her passengers hanging on with skilled expertise. "Hurry!" screamed Robert, his voice shrill. The wind blew his straw hat off but he did not even look back.

Every time that Rachel looked back over her shoulders she saw how much faster the rebel riders were traveling. Then, when she looked towards Gettysburg, the frightened girl still saw how far it was to the town. As soon as Rachel heard the jingling of the Confederates' equipment she knew they were not going to get away.

Moments later the fastest of the riders caught up with them and reached out with a gloved hand and grabbed Nutmeg's bridle. The wildly bearded horseman pulled back on his mount and brought both horses to a frightening halt. The other rebels came to a stop, surrounding the youths. Dust plumed high into the air.

Rachel glanced from rider to rider, her face white with alarm. There were six Southerners, their clothes caked with dust, and their faces raw from sunburn. The men smelled of sweat, horse, leather, and unwashed bodies. Rachel bit at her lips to keep her teeth from chattering. She was determined to not let them know she was afraid.

Once the horses had settled down, the rider who had stopped them let go of Nutmeg's bridle. The mare flicked its head about angrily but could not go anywhere, as the soldiers had crowded around and hemmed her in. Rachel's brown eyes darted from Confederate to Confederate, trying to find out which one was their leader. When Rachel fixed her vision upon a handsome young soldier, his dark eyes sparkled in merriment.

"Good afternoon, Miss," the elegant one said, taking his hat off and bowing. He looked up, tried to knock the dust from his hat, and then fitted it back up onto his head. "It's my pleasure to meet you."

"What do you want?" Rachel bit out harshly.

"Why, ma'am, where are your manners? I was not aware that you Northern ladies were so rude."

Rachel's heart was hammering inside her chest, a beat so loud she was convinced the Confederates could hear. But she kept her chin up and glared at the handsome one. He smiled again, showing white teeth from between sun-chapped lips.

"What should we do with 'em, Lieutenant?" asked a rider with a huge drooping mustache. But the young officer ignored his trooper and continued to smile at the girls.

"You remind me of my sister, back home in Atlanta." Several of the riders chuckled.

"Yes," agreed one with long ratty hair, "she do remind me of your sister, Julie. Why that one's a hellcat, if I ever met one." The riders were now all smiling at the thought of the lieutenant's sister.

"Woe be it to the man what weds with George's sister." All of the troopers laughed loudly, and traded grins among themselves. "She may be a first-rate beauty, but she's as wild as an Injun squaw."

"Now there will be no disrespecting of my sister, Julie. She's just got a mild temper and is a little on the untamed side."

"Mild temper?" one questioned.

"Untamed side! Lieutenant," another said. "Why that she-cat could scratch the eyes out of a wild bear and sing and smile while do'un so." The men laughed again and then were quiet. They looked from Rachel to Annie, and back to their young officer.

"So, Lieutenant, what do we do with them? If we let 'em go they'll run into town and tell everybody we're here."

"I guess we'll have to take 'em back with us," suggested another.

"No!" cried Annie. With that, Robert leaped from the back of Nutmeg, dodged between the legs of the Confederates' horses, and sprinted towards Gettysburg.

"Look at that little chickabiddy run!" laughed the men.

"Want me to go get him?" asked another.

The lieutenant looked at Robert, the eight-year-old running as fast as he could, and then shook his head. "No. Who's going to believe the words of a terrified tadpole."

"But what we gonna do with the ladies? They's old enough to know what's happ'nun."

The officer turned to the white-faced Rachel and asked, "How old are you, Miss?"

Rachel straightened up to her full height and glared at the handsome soldier. "That is none of your business, sir." Some of the men chuckled when the young lieutenant's face reddened, but their hilarity died quickly when an errant artillery shell exploded a quarter mile away.

"I think that's Heth's boys over there, Charlie," said the one who had captured Nutmeg. "They're fighting a whole passel of Yankees. There's a hell of a lot more over there than just some Pennsylvania militia. Pardon my language there, Missy."

"Yep," said the mangy bearded one. "We better be gett'un a message back to the colonel 'bout this here road into town. It don't look like nobody knows we's a com'un."

"Right, Sam," said the lieutenant. "Go back, quick as you can and tell the colonel the road's empty, and that if he hurries, the brigade can catch the Yankees from behind. And Andy, you go with him."

"Right!" With that both riders galloped off, whipping at their tired and lathered horses.

"Now, Missy," said the lieutenant, his face softening as he turned towards the two cousins. "Can I have your word that you will tell no one about us being here?"

"Yes, sir," Rachel whispered as she nodded, but vowed to herself that she was going to notify the sheriff, just as soon as they got into Gettysburg. The rebel frowned. Maybe, thought Rachel, he had been able to read her mind.

"Charlie, I don't know if it's a good idea to believe the promises of this Northern filly," cautioned one of the dust-covered riders.

"No, you may be right," agreed the handsome lieutenant, "but I certainly don't want to take her back." He ran his fingers through his dusty beard, trying to figure out what he was going to do.

"Charlie," said the mangy bearded one, "that Missy's mount is in a whole lot better condition than mine. Why don't we just take her fine mare, here, and be on our way."

"No!" screamed Annie, clinging to Nutmeg's mane.

"Yep, Lieutenant," said another, "iffen we takes the mount, your two little girlfriends, here, why they'll have to walk back to town. That'll give the brigade time to come on up and catch the whole Yankee army from behind."

Another added, "It ain't no skin off our backs to let 'em go. Hell, we can't feed 'em. I say we just take the mare and leave 'em here."

"We could use another mount, especially one that's in such good condition."

The young officer thought for a few more seconds and then nodded. "Take the horse."

With that, one of the riders reached in and grasped Rachel and lifted her off Nutmeg. She squirmed and kicked but could do nothing. Another grabbed Annie and raised her up. She screamed and bit the Confederate's arm. He howled in pain and dropped her onto the ground. Annie fell with a thud and lay stunned.

"Let's go," commanded the officer. The Southerners turned and rode away, taking Nutmeg with them. Annie sat up, pleading for them to come back, but soon realized her appeals were being ignored. The Confederates galloped away, taking Annie's mare with them. The distraught girl began to sob.

Rachel knelt down next to her wailing cousin and hugged her, but Annie continued to cry. Nutmeg was the treasure of Annie's life and to have her horse ripped out from beneath her was a catastrophe. The red-haired girl moaned tearfully, laying amid the dust on the road.

Once Annie cried herself out, Rachel was able to get her up and begin walking towards home. Then, Rachel noticed how quiet the countryside had become. When she looked towards the west the low, gray clouds of gun smoke were gone and the afternoon had become still. Rachel sighed, hoping the battle was over.

When the two distraught girls reached the Diamond they encountered a long column of blue-coated infantry soldiers. These dusty and tired men wore red, moon-shaped badges on their hats. Rachel rushed up to the first mounted officer she could find and told him about the Confederates that she had seen. The weary soldier thanked her, and then continued on his way.

Rachel and Annie staggered back to the Kendall house and collapsed on the kitchen chairs. While Rachel told their story Annie resumed her tears. Both cousins' mothers grew ashen faced when they heard what had happened. They had not been able to make much sense out of what Robert had said, other than that Rachel had been yelling at him. He also had failed to mention that they had been caught by a group of Confederates.

Annie's mother, Mary Taylor, put on her shawl and hat and went out, furiously searching for someone who would go and retrieve her daughter's horse. She wished her husband, John, was not in Harrisburg, purchasing new school books. Mary needed her husband now, but he was not here. Thus, the furious woman had to go hunting for an officer who would know how to bring Nutmeg back to them.

Annie, her face streaked with tears, her eyes red from crying, could not stop her weeping. In time, Francis Kendall mixed some laudanum with water and gave it to her to drink. The troubled girl drank the bitter-tasting potion and was led upstairs to Rachel's room. It only took a few minutes before the drug took effect, and she fell asleep.

Chapter 8

The Confederates Attack

When Ben learned that Johnny had been shot he groaned in anguish. The dream had been correct. Ben immediately felt guilty because he had done nothing to prevent what he knew was going to happen. The youth wandered off by himself and leaned up against a cedar tree. His close friend was hurt.

Ben pounded his fist against the bark of the cedar. He could not remember the first time he had ever met Johnny. The two had grown up together, as the Baker farmstead abutted the property owned by Ben's father. Johnny and Ben had done everything together. The two had sweated in the summer's heat, splitting rails, cutting hay, and hoeing weeds. They had also been partners in crime at school, thrown rocks at innocent milk cows, and stolen watermelons from Sam Williams' fields. Ben shook his head in anguish. Now, Johnny was being carried away to some field hospital. The young soldier slumped down and sat, leaning against the pithy tree trunk.

Sergeant Daughterly had told them where Johnny had been found, and because the teenagers were combat veterans, the older man did not sugar coat Baker's injury. He briefly described Johnny's wound and predicted the youth's foot would have to be amputated. Ben groaned sadly, knowing that a boy having only one foot would be of little use to a farmer. After the amputation, the army would send Johnny home, a cripple, who would never be able to play baseball again.

Why, thought Ben, was his friend wounded while he sat here, under the shade of this cedar? The two had been standing, side-by-side, when the bullet cut Johnny down. Ben took a deep breath and pounded at the dirt with his fist. He was ashamed of himself for not realizing his friend had fallen, just inches away, and he had gone on, leaving Johnny behind.

Ben wondered if Johnny was afraid, then shook his head. His friend feared nothing, not getting into a fight with a bigger foe, or being whipped by his Pa, or jumping into a pen filled with terrorized hogs. Johnny did not have nightmares caused by the shock of battle, like Ben did. Nor did he tremble before the regiment went into a fight. He just stuck out his chin, squinted his eyes, and muttered, "Come on, give me your best shot!" But a rebel bullet had cut Johnny down, ripping his foot away, mutilating him, and leaving him crippled for life.

"Ben, how's it going?"

The young blacksmith looked up and saw the gentle eyes of Lieutenant East. The officer knelt down on one knee and patted Ben on the shoulder. The boy reached up and touched East's hand. A river of calmness flowed into the unsettled youth's body and he closed his eyes.

"We've all seen this before, the loss of a close friend," said the lieutenant. "But this is not a permanent loss, Johnny's going to be all right. Oh, he'll be on crutches because of his stump, but Ben, your friend is tough. He'll get through this. Johnny will be home in Selma in no time, chasing after Rebecca Williams."

Ben's head snapped up and he glared at Lieutenant East. Ben's mind whirled. Johnny had better not be spending time with Rebecca, she was promised to him.

Then, the youth saw East's smile. "I was only teasing," he said quietly. "Everybody knows that Rebecca's waiting for you to come home."

"Yes she is," Ben stated firmly.

"But the point I was making is that your friend will survive and adjust to his disability. He's a smart lad, though he wasn't the best of students. Johnny'll figure out what he can do and turn that keen mind of his into making a profit. And then he'll notice Sarah Benning."

"Sarah Benning?"

"That's right, just you wait and see."

"How did you know about Sarah?"

Lieutenant East chuckled. "Oh, a teacher has to watch everyone very carefully. It's a survival requirement, you know."

"Oh?"

"Yes." Lieutenant East patted Ben's shoulder and added, "I just got a letter from Sarah, inquiring whether she thought Johnny would consent to exchanging letters with her."

"You did, really? When?"

"Last night, we had mail call while you guys were out, stealing the local farmers blind." East paused, glancing off to the north to watch the explosions from a distant barrage of artillery shells. He took off his big black hat and ran his hand through his hair. "I just didn't have time to talk to Johnny today."

"Did I get any mail?"

"I think so, but you'll have to see the first sergeant. But right now he's pretty busy so don't go and pester him. There will be time tonight." Lieutenant East stood up and looked down at the young teen. "So, Private Ellis, you had better be careful, and follow orders."

"Yes, sir."

"And remember, Johnny will be okay. Oh, it'll be a while before he's home and chasing after Sarah, but he'll make it. Do you cotton to what I'm saying?"

"Yeah."

"Good." The lieutenant reached down to give Ben a hand up, "Now get back where you are supposed to be. I think Bobby Lee's boys are up to something and we need every rifle we can get."

"Thank you, sir." With that, Ben began walking back to where the company was resting.

"Oh, and Ben."

"Yes?"

"I still will be watching you and Sam. As of yet I haven't returned the favor for what you did to me, back in school. You know—the hornets?" The two laughed.

Ben sat with Sam for the next 30 minutes, resting, and talking about their morning's fight. It had been brief, noisy, and terrifying. The two were glad to be alive. Now, they, along with everyone else in the regiment, waited to see what the Confederates were going to do.

Later, a commotion caused the boys to look up. The boys groaned when they saw the reb forces forming to attack. "Look," whispered Sam, his voice hushed by the magnitude of the Southerner's formation. The gray lines stretched for at least three-quarters of a mile. The Indianans moved into their ranks without being given any orders. The veterans stood and stared at the Confederates who slowly marched towards their position.

The Southerners outnumbered the small Indiana regiment. Ben counted four red-and-white Confederate battle flags. That meant there were four regiments bearing down on the 19th Indiana.

"Guess we're going to have to fight them," declared the corporal who stood at Ben's right shoulder.

"Sure are a lot of 'em," another Indianan uttered.

Ben turned to Sam and the two looked into each other's eyes. They had been friends a long time and found it hard to believe that Johnny was not standing next to them. This would be the first time in two years that the three had not gone into a fight together. Ben tried to wet his lips and frowned because his mouth was so dry. His heart pounded and when he looked down at his hands, he found them to be trembling.

"Hold steady, boys," said Lieutenant East. "Let not your heart be troubled, believe in God."

"There are too many of them! We ought to pull back," one of the anxious soldiers wailed.

"No," countered East, "it is not possible for this cup to pass us by." The lieutenant gazed at the menacing force coming towards them and swallowed, his Adam's apple moving up and down. "There is no greater love than for a man to lay down his life for his friends."

Ben's knees quivered. He tried to make the shaking stop but could not. The youth glanced out of the corner of his eye to see how Sam was doing. The young soldier was white faced and quiet, his vision locked on the ponderous force coming at them.

"Ben," Sam whispered, "I'm scared." This confession shocked Ben, but also gave him courage. Their friendship could not be tainted, nor could it be broken.

"Me too," Ben confided.

The rebel force was now about three hundred yards away, slowly marching across a wheat field. The boys had never seen so many Confederates all at one time. It looked like the entire Southern army was aimed straight at them. Colonel Williams had posted a company of skirmishers out in front of the regiment. These boys popped up from their hiding places and started shooting. The gray line was not affected and crept perilously closer to the Yanks.

"Hold steady," hissed Lieutenant East. He moved among the company, patting boys on the shoulders. "They're just as scared as we are."

The skirmishers had done all they could, but the Confederates continued to approach. The officer in charge of the skirmishers gave the order for his boys to retire and they leaped up and raced back towards the 19th Indiana's defenses.

"It's our turn next," whimpered a frightened trooper.

"The sun will be darkened, and the moon will not give its light," uttered Lieutenant East.

"We got to get out of here, they'll kill us all!"

"Heaven and earth will pass away, but His words will not."

The shooting began at the right end of the regiment and quickly spread all along the line. Ben's musket slammed into his shoulder when he pulled the trigger. The smoke from more than 250 rifles billowed out in front of the soldiers. That first volley slammed into the approaching Confederate line, striking dozens of men. Some just pitched forward and fell face forward into the wheat. Others toppled over backwards. There also were some who clutched at their wounds, staggered briefly, and then slumped to the ground.

The youth quickly began to reload. Again, the right side of the regiment was first to fire, and the shooting moved down the line as the soldiers completed reloading. More Southerners fell into the trampled and blood-splattered wheat.

Those first two volleys punished the Confederates and forced the rebels to give up on their thoughts of advancing. The gray-coats halted and began to reform their lines. Ben could see file closers moving men forward to fill in the gaps. Then the Southerners began to return fire.

Bullets zipped over Ben's head, buzzing angrily. A Yank a few yards off to his left groaned and toppled forward. The youth raised his rifle and fired again, the

blast ringing in his ears. Ben's world was reduced to
nothing more than loading and shooting.

Time seemed to stand still. Ben had become a
thoughtless machine. He loaded and fired, not wondering where his bullets were going, not caring if they
struck their targets. Around the youth, his comrades
loaded and fired. Some cursed and yelled, others muttered prayers. Here and there, a soldier would grunt
and then slump to the ground. Others already lay at
their feet; some silent and still, while many moaned
or screamed.

Ben was surprised when he reached into his cartridge box and discovered that it was empty. The young
veteran had not realized how quickly he had fired his
20 rounds. He stepped back from the firing line and
began to transfer bullets from the bottom of the cartridge box to the top. As Ben was doing this Sam
coughed, grabbed at his belly, and stumbled backwards. Sam turned sideways and fell to the ground.
Ben immediately stopped what he was doing, grabbed
his friend, and dragged him behind a tree. Once they
were behind the maple, Ben knelt beside his friend.

"Ben," Sam sobbed, "they shot me!" He clutched
at his belly, his eyes wide with fear.

"Let me see," ordered Ben. He pulled Sam's hands
away from his friend's stomach as he coughed and
moaned.

"Oh, Lordy, they shot me!"

But Ben did not see any blood. In fact, he could
not even find a bullet hole in Sam's blue wool coat.
Then the teenager saw Sam's problem and laughed in
relief.

"Look, you hornswoggle, the bullet hit your belt
buckle."

"Huh?"

"Yeah, you're not hurt. Your belt buckle stopped
the ball. You're going to be okay."

"What?"

"So, get up and quit whining."

"But it hurts so bad!"

"I bet so. But you're not hurt."

"Oh." With that Sam sat up and tenderly rubbed his stomach. He then inspected his belt buckle. The tarnished brass "US" had been bent but it had stopped a musket ball. The bullet was mashed against the buckle, a glob of gray against the brass's golden color. "Well, I'll be doggone."

Just then a bullet ripped through Ben's coattail, cutting a round hole. The youth was quickly reminded of the danger lurking just beyond the safety of the tree trunk. The youth crawled forward and picked up his rifle.

Ben finished filling his cartridge box and then re-loaded his weapon. Bullets slammed into the tree, knocking away leaves and bark. The youth found that he did not want to leave the tree trunk's protection. So, he stayed behind the big maple.

The company battle line was just a few feet in front of the tree. Many of the soldiers were kneeling, loading, and firing as quickly as they were able. A few though, remained standing, preferring the added risk so they could load more quickly than their kneeling comrades. There also had to be more than a dozen who were now down. When Ben looked from his company to the others in the regiment, he saw the same horrible results. Each company was marked by a line of wounded and dead who lay at the feet of their surviving comrades.

"What are you doing back here?" shouted Lieutenant East. "I'll have no skulkers in my company!" The officer grabbed Ben by the collar and yanked him from behind the tree and pushed him up to the firing line. "Now kill somebody!" he yelled.

Ben fired without aiming and then knelt down, cringing as a bullet smacked into the person next to him. Blood and tissue splattered over his arms and hands. He wiped at the sticky stuff and then began to reload. But his hands were shaking so badly he could not hold onto the paper cartridge. The round tumbled from his fingers and fell to the ground.

Ben reached into his cartridge box and retrieved another bullet. He successfully recharged his Springfield, directed it towards the rebel lines, and fired. The weapon recoiled into Ben's shoulder. The boy then grabbed another cartridge. He loaded and fired repeatedly for several more minutes.

"All right now," shouted Lieutenant East, "Fall back! Fall back!" The officer pulled at the survivors in the company, jerking them away from the firing line and pushing them towards the right. The soldiers quickly began to follow the others who were running towards a ravine.

Ben did not hear the lieutenant's orders, and continued to load and shoot. A bullet coming from the left struck the boy's black hat, drilling two large holes. The big hat never moved.

"Lordy," shouted Lieutenant East, "Ben Ellis, we don't need any more dead heroes. You get back here!" But the officer saw that the teenager did not hear him so he darted forward and grabbed the youth. He pulled Ben backwards and spun him around.

The haze cleared from Ben's eyes and he saw what had happened. The regiment's battle line had been shot to pieces, and then flanked from the left. The survivors were now all running towards a ravine that led towards a low, tree-covered hill. The Confederates howled as they pursued the retreating blue-coats.

"Follow me, and go to our colors!" shouted Lieutenant East. The officer turned to see if Ben was following and saw that the boy was right on his heels. East dashed from tree to tree as Confederate bullets zipped past him, or smacked against nearby tree trunks. Lieutenant East called to other Hoosiers who huddled behind logs, or cringed behind trees. A few of them rose up and followed after their leader.

As Ben ran behind the lieutenant, the boy yelled at the scared soldiers, ordering them to follow him. The men, encouraged by both East and Ellis, overcame their fear and scampered after them. Soon the officer had a dozen men trailing right behind him.

"Good work, Ellis!" East shouted. "Now, to the colors." The officer raced towards a clump of soldiers who clustered around the regiment's precious flags. Ben saw that Sergeant Major Asa Blanchard was holding the regimental colors and heard him shout, "Rally, boys, rally!"

More Hoosiers gathered about the flags. Sergeants and officers spread the men out and pushed them into a firing line. The Indiana veterans began to shoot into the screaming Confederates. Again, gray-clad soldiers began to drop. Lieutenant East pointed to a space next to a rotting stump and Ben crouched down behind it. The panting youth reloaded his rifle and then pointed it at the rebs. The weapon bucked against his shoulder.

The intensity of their fire slowed the Confederates, and the Southerners sought shelter behind trees and logs. The battle-seasoned rebs returned fire. Bullets zipped and hissed past the boys in their new position. Other chunks of lead thudded into trees or struck human flesh. Ben continued loading and shooting.

Sergeant Major Blanchard crumpled to the ground, the national flag falling from his hands. The wounded Hoosier rolled over on his side, clutching at his thigh. Blood spurted from his leg and pooled on the ground beneath him, and stained the silken folds of the precious red-white-and-blue banner. He tried to stop the bleeding but the main artery had been severed. Asa cried out for help, but soon his calls weakened as the blood drained from his body.

"Get the flag!" shouted a captain.

"No," argued Lieutenant East. "It's too dangerous. Too many people have already gone down."

"But we can't leave the colors to the Johnnies," complained the officer.

"No," continued Lieutenant East, "roll up the colors and get them out of sight." With that, East crawled forward and picked the flag up and began to wrap it around the staff. The captain saw the sense in what the ex-teacher was doing and went to help him.

Bullets kicked up dirt around the two officers, causing them to flinch and cower downwards. But seconds later the two resolute men continued rolling up the American flag. Ben was loading his rifle when a bullet struck Lieutenant East squarely in the back of his head. The officer dropped without uttering a sound. The captain, surprised that East had been killed, just inches from where he knelt, grabbed the flag by its staff and began to crawl away.

The regiment's other flag, the blue regimental, a fighting eagle emblazoned upon it, also fell to the ground when rebel riflemen concentrated their fire upon the brave man holding it. Someone shouted to pick up the large standard but no one would. Now, as the unsettled Indiana soldiers had nothing to rally around, some of the more cautious men began to drift backwards, abandoning the defensive line.

"Raise those colors!" shouted the hearty voice of Colonel Williams. But no one would pick up the hazardous banner.

"I'll do it!" shouted Ben. The boy set down his rifle and sprinted to where the regimental flag lay. He snatched the colors from the ground and waved it in the air, high above his head.

"Bully for Ellis!" somebody shouted, and several others took up the cheer.

"Pour it into them!" hollered an officer, seeing the effect the raised colors had upon the infantrymen. "We can hold this line. Yes we can!" The Hoosiers increased their fire, knocking down several Confederates who had crept close to the Union position.

A bullet zipped close to Ben's ear, buzzing like an angry bee. Another projectile plucked at his sleeve, cutting away the light blue piping at the cuff, and shattering a brass button. Then, two bullets cut holes in Ben's coat tails. He could not see the balls coming at him, but the youth could hear their perilous passage. Ben continued to wave the flag and scream words of encouragement to his comrades.

The bullet that struck Ben came from his left, rather than from straight ahead. The huge slug smacked into his right hand exactly where he had it clamped around the flagstaff. The .58-caliber bullet severed Ben's third and fourth fingers almost as neatly as if someone had taken a hatchet and chopped them off. His little finger was shredded with bone chips and splinters from the flagpole. Blood and pieces of finger tissue splashed across Ben's face.

The flag fell from Ben's grip and toppled to the earth. The stunned boy stood frozen, more bullets zipping past him. "Son, what have they done to you?" cried Colonel Williams.

"I've been shot," Ben said woodenly. He held his smashed right hand with his left, staring at the shiny blood flowing down his arm.

"Get him down!" someone shouted, and firm hands reached out and yanked Ben down behind a bullet-ridden log.

"I'll help you," said another. The Hoosier pulled out a scarf and wrapped it around Ben's injured hand. "There," he announced, "it's almost good as new."

"Ben Ellis," called out Colonel Williams, "you are wounded."

"Oh, it's just a little scratch," mumbled the shocked boy.

"I want you to go to the rear and have that hand looked after," commanded the officer. When he saw that Ben was slow to move, he shouted, "Ellis, I said get out of here, now!"

Ben nodded his head and crawled away from the log. Then, when he was 10 yards away his legs gained strength, he stood up and raced from the danger of the battle line. The youth ran swiftly, now that fear had taken control. The boy bolted between the trees and up the hill. He soon was over the top of the ridge and down into the shallow valley on the other side.

Suddenly, the frightening noises of battle were left behind. All that Ben could hear were the far-off sounds of musketry. No longer could he discern the frenzied humming of bullets, nor the sounds of lead striking trees, logs, earth, or human flesh. He stumbled and fell, his legs suddenly becoming wobbly.

Ben rolled onto his back, gasping for air, his heart pounding as loud as a battery of cannons. But slowly his breathing and pulse returned to normal. His will-power began to take control, and the fear was pushed back into the deeper recess of his brain. Ben knew he was no longer in danger. Oh, he had been wounded, but he knew from experience that the injury was not nearly serious enough to be lethal. Unless, he thought with a slash of worry, it should get infected. Ben realized he must get up and go to the surgeons. They could take care of his hand.

Chapter 9

Confusion in Town

Ben walked cautiously across the open pasture—
the same one the regiment had crossed, earlier this
morning. Only then, the 19th Indiana had numbered
almost three hundred. Now, he guessed there might
be less than half still with Colonel Williams. He followed other walking wounded who were slowly making their way towards the Lutheran Seminary.

When Ben reached the front of the stone and brick
building he found it crowded with wagons, ambulances,
buggies, and uncounted numbers of wounded soldiers.
After searching around for a few minutes, Ben found
Doctor Abraham Haines, the 19th Indiana's assistant
surgeon. The harried physician, his apron and arms
splattered with blood, glanced at the youth and shook
his head.

"Son," he muttered wearily, "I don't have time for
you. Your injury is much too trifling for me to waste
time on you here. There are way too many seriously
injured boys who need my services."

"Oh."

"That's right, lad. I want you to walk on into town.
Find the train station. That's where Ebersole is. He'll
have the time to deal with you."

"The train station?"

"That's right. Just ask when you get there. The townspeople will know where it is. And Jake Ebersole will do you up fine. Now, get going, I don't have any more time to waste talking to you."

"The train station?"

"That's right." The surgeon turned his back on Ben and leaned over a screaming soldier. He looked back over his shoulder and called out, "Good luck, lad."

Ben shook his head, trying to get the ringing in his ears to stop. He walked away from the seminary building and soon found his way onto the Chambersburg Pike, and stepped slowly towards town. His hand hurt something fierce now. Ben discovered if he kept the hand elevated that lessened the pain, as well as slowing the bleeding.

Not only was there heavy gunfire coming from the west, where the regiment was, there also was now serious sounds of fighting off to the north of Gettysburg. Huge clouds of smoke and dust boiled up in a massive half circle, stretching probably two miles, going from west to north, and then towards the east. The rumble of cannon and musketry rolled across the Pennsylvania landscape.

Chambersburg Pike was crowded with vehicles, riders, and a stream of walking wounded. No one knew what was going on, however each man moved to his own needs, and Ben was but one speck in this flood of movement. He passed a fellow who lay beside the road, crying for his mother. Ben stared at him for a moment. The soldier had been gut shot and someone had stuffed a towel over the man's stomach but this did little to stop the leakage of blood and intestines. Ben did not stop.

When Ben reached the western outskirts of town he saw civilians crammed together, up on top of a store building. They were watching the fighting, pointing and chatting merrily. He shook his head. Those townsfolk would not be so happy if they were out there, where he had been.

"Are you thirsty, soldier?" asked a heavyset woman. The huge lady astonished Ben, as he had not seen her until she spoke. The boy rubbed his eyes, surprised that his vision had become hazy. He nodded slowly, suddenly remembering just how parched his throat was. She dipped a cup into a bucket of water and handed it to him. Ben gulped the liquid down, savoring the mineral taste, and handed her the cup. The sad-faced woman looked into his eyes and saw his craving, so she filled the tin again and thrust it back to him. Ben consumed the second cup just as quickly as the first.

"That's all for now," she said. "There's more thirsty boys coming." The woman then pushed past Ben and approached two other wounded soldiers. "Are you thirsty?" she asked them.

Ben reached out and touched her shoulder. She turned in amazement. "I said, that's all you get," she growled.

"Where's the train station?"

"Oh, you want to know where to go?" Ben nodded. "All the wounded boys are going to Christ Lutheran Church. Of course that's getting pretty full now. I heard they're also taking boys to the courthouse. That's on the corner of Middle and Baltimore. It's easy to find. Just turn right at the next corner." With that she moved away from Ben, handing out more water.

Ben rubbed his eyes with his good hand and shuffled along the street. The lady had said to go to the courthouse but Doctor Haines had said the regiment's hospital was at the train station. Well, Ben did not know where the train station was, but he did have directions to the courthouse. The weary youth continued slowly on his way.

Just as the woman had said, the courthouse was easy to find. In fact, lots of hurt men were headed towards that building. When Ben arrived he was dismayed to find that hundreds of other wounded men had already gotten here before him. The sidewalks surrounding the brick building were clogged with injured soldiers, some moaning and sobbing, others just laying quietly, stoically enduring their travails. A harried assistant came out of the front door carrying two pails of severed hands and feet. He dumped them onto a smelly pile of amputated parts. Ben grabbed at the man's arm.

"Where's the train station?" the youth asked hoarsely. The medical assistant shrugged off Ben's hand but answered, "Go north on Baltimore, past the diamond. You can't miss it. Now, leave me alone. Can't you see I'm busy." With that the man rushed back up the steps and disappeared into the building.

Ben turned around and stumbled away from the courthouse. He was not going to get any medical attention here. The boy slowly worked his way through the confusion filling Gettysburg's major north-south thoroughfare, and came to the main intersection. A regimental band was playing patriotic music, all of the brass instruments shining in the summer sun. Ben was so tired that he slumped down next to a wooden barrel and leaned against it. He dozed off. When Ben awoke, the youth did not know how long he had slept, however, the intersection was not jammed with vehicles and soldiers, and the brass band was no longer playing melodies. Ben painfully stood up, weaving back and forth as he struggled for balance, and then stumbled northwards.

The exhausted youth found the train station a few minutes later. The building was a small, two-story brick building with a bell tower on its roof. Wounded soldiers lay along the sidewalks and underneath a long, wooden porch. Ben recognized Doctor Ebersole and stumbled towards him.

The busy surgeon saw the "19" on Ben's black hat and motioned to him. "You're one of my boys," he announced flatly. Ben nodded. "Well, as you can see I'm really busy here." While the surgeon talked, he continued to work on a soldier, who moaned at Ben's feet.

"Just from looking at you I'd say your wound is insignificant." The injured soldier at Ben's feet groaned loudly and jerked. "Hold still, I say!" shouted Ebersole. "You want me to help you or just tear things apart?" The doctor worked on the wounded man for a few minutes and then swore in frustration. He turned, looking for an orderly and when he found none, called out loudly, "Would somebody get this dead man out of here!"

Jacob Ebersole wiped at the blood on his face and focused on Ben. "Well, son, I don't have time to deal with you right now. The boys just keep coming in, and most of them are hurt a whole lot worse than you. Now, if you want, you can wait awhile. Maybe, if things slow down, I can get to you later."

"Well, Doctor Haines told me to come here."

"He did, did he? Well, go tell Haines that I don't need him to refer me any new patients. There's a whole bunch of Iron Brigade fellows already here, so you're not alone." Ebersole moved on to the next wounded soldier on the blood-splattered wooden floor. The injured boy struggled as soon as the physician touched him. "Hold still, son, or it's going to be a lot worse."

"What should I do?" Ben asked wearily.

"Wait. Or go some place else. I'm real busy here and you're not going to die." The surgeon paused what he was doing and looked at Ben. "I don't want to sound callous, son, especially since you are one of my boys. But, you'll be all right. However, there are many who need my immediate attention, or they could die. You're in much better shape than they are. Do you understand?"

"Oh." With that, Ben shuffled away and found himself a place to lay down. Ben's hand throbbed, his head ached, he was horribly thirsty, and he was so very tired. He drifted off to sleep.

Later, Ben was shaken awake by a hospital steward wearing a "19" on his hat. "Hey, boy," said the male nurse, "how you doing?" Ben tried to answer but his mouth felt as if it was filled with cotton. "I think I know you, you're one of the Selma boys aren't you?"

Ben nodded. "Yeah, I thought so. I'm from Muncie. I've been to Selma many times. I'm Henry Marsh, I don't know if we've ever met. If you had been sick or something I would know all about you but it's plain to see that you're not a new recruit so you must have been pretty healthy, and lucky, too."

"Uh-huh."

"How you holding up?"

"My hand hurts pretty bad."

"Yeah, I imagine it does, but you'll be okay. You got to listen to me though, things have gone from bad to worse while you were sleeping. If you can walk, I suggest you get out of here."

"What?"

"Yeah, the whole XI Corps has broken. It looks like we're going to lose the town."

"Lose the town?"

"That's right, sonny. Old Howard's boys aren't worth the price of a three-legged horse." The nurse wiped at the sweat on his forehead with a blood-covered hand. He looked to the north, a worried look in his eyes. "If the Johnnies take the town they'll round up every man who's not hurt bad—and I mean boys like you. They'll march you off to prison. So, if you can, I suggest you get out of here."

"I'm so thirsty," Ben croaked.

"I'll get you some water, then you high tail it out of here. Sorry I can't do much else for you." The hospital steward brought Ben a ladle filled with water. The youth gulped the liquid down. "Now, you get out of here. And be careful!"

Ben stumbled back to Gettysburg's Diamond. It was now a chaotic mess of wagons, shuffling wounded soldiers, riders, panicked men, and debris. Frightened troops were rushing into the main intersection, coming from the west and from the north. The noise was tremendous; the fear was infectious. Ben could see that the army was collapsing around him.

There was no place to go so he wearily made his way back to the courthouse. By now the sidewalks were packed with wounded, and the sounds of pain and agony created a mournful din. Ben could go no farther, but he did not want to remain out on the streets, so he slowly made his way around to the back of the building and found a way to get inside.

Once indoors, the youth crept past the throngs of wounded soldiers and entered a large room. The chamber was filled with badly hurt troops. Cries and groans echoed off the wooden walls. Blood was pooled in places on the floors. Flies buzzed everywhere. The hot room reeked of unwashed bodies, blood, urine, and excrement. But Ben could go no farther.

The worn-out boy searched the benches to see if there was a place to lay down but the seats for every pew were filled. He stumbled over a wounded man and fell, landing on his injured hand. Ben cried out in pain. However, he noticed that there was space to lay down, underneath the pew. The teen crawled into this haven, beneath the seat of a wooden bench. The hardwood planking was just what the boy wanted. Ben quickly fell asleep.

Chapter 10

The Escape

Sam was following a pack of soldiers, running for all he was worth. The collapse had come so quickly he had been astounded. Colonel Williams had led what was left of the 19th Indiana out of the woods and across that wide pasture in which the regiment had advanced, hours earlier. The colonel then placed the Hoosiers behind a barricade of logs and rails.

The regiment had been badly hurt. Company K had about half of its original strength left, and only Captain Orr as the remaining officer. The men were tired, thirsty, and shocked by the sudden violence that had fallen onto their comrades and friends. They were discouraged by their losses but Colonel Williams would not let them dwell on the terrible things that had happened. The big man forced the Indianans to clean their weapons, reinforce the rail barricade, and prepare for the next expected Confederate assault.

The rebels were not in a hurry to attack again, so other regiments were able to take up position next to the 19th Indiana. Then, two batteries of artillery moved in and unlimbered their big steel and brass weapons. It did not take long for the worn-down Hoosiers to realize that their new position was one of considerable strength.

When the Confederates did storm over the distant ridge and rush towards the Union line they quickly learned of the power which the Federals had assembled. The infantrymen and artillery shattered one brigade composed of five regiments. The decimated survivors fell back to the safety of a fence line, a quarter mile away after just 15 minutes of slaughter. When the gray-clad soldiers withdrew they left behind a pasture strewn with hundreds of wrecked and mangled bodies. One soldier proclaimed, "Their ranks went down like grass before the scythe."

A few minutes later Colonel Williams called the 19th's officers together and told them it was time to retreat. At first, when Captain Orr relayed the order to the boys in Company K, his boys wanted to argue. After all, they had just helped whip an entire brigade of Johnnies. But then, as they saw that other Federal units were beginning to break away from the rail barricades, they realized their defensive position was falling apart. The Indianans soon heard rumors telling of a terrible disaster. The men learned that the XI Corps, north of Gettysburg, had broken and run, leaving them in danger of being surrounded. The veterans quickly understood their situation; if they did not fall back they stood a very good chance of being captured.

Then, panic set in and the formation dissolved, every man for himself. Sam trailed along behind some of the other fellows in the company, but soon lost track of them in the confusion on Chambersburg Pike. There were now so many soldiers streaming back to Gettysburg that Sam seldom even saw a brother black-hat from the Iron Brigade. As he neared town the congestion increased and the mob's flight slowed.

"Sam! Sam!" a familiar voice shouted. The youth looked around among the sea of scared faces but saw no one he recognized. "Up here, Bradshaw," the speaker yelled. Looking up, Sam spotted Captain Orr and raised his hand to let the officer know he had seen him, and Orr pointed to a small group of Company K boys who were clustered together in the doorway of a shop. Sam crashed his way through the mass of soldiers and joined the group.

"Those people are crazy," said a big Selma farm boy.

"Yes," agreed Captain Orr, "and they're all going to be captured if they keep going where they're headed. The rebs are pushing us from the west and from the north. They're flushing us out like hounds at a pheasant hunt. I want you all to stay with me. We'll use our wits and work our way through town. We're supposed to meet back at some cemetery on the southeast part of town. I intend to get there and bring my company with me. Are you ready?" The men nodded. "Good, well then, follow me."

The officer made a right turn onto Washington Street and headed south. His little band of followers stayed right on his heels. Though there were lots of panicked soldiers on this route the congestion was not nearly as bad as out on Chambersburg Street.

A little while later the group came to a mob of soldiers who gathered around a well. Sam was as thirsty as the rest of the boys in the company and crowded in, trying to get his empty canteen filled. The parched blue-coats pushed and shoved, trying to get at the well. Then an artillery round exploded against the side of a brick house, barely 10 yards from the rabble. Broken brick, glass, and shrapnel sprayed the multitude and many fell to the dusty earth. The rest began to stampede down the street, howling as they ran.

Captain Orr shouted above the cursing and wailing and called to his Selma boys. The officer led them off the dangerous street and into an alley. Bullets buzzed down the length of the street, struck human flesh, or "thwacked" against the wooden planks of frame houses. Sam looked behind the little group and saw a group of Confederates chasing after them.

"Follow me!" shouted Orr. He leaped over a picket fence and raced past an outhouse and a chicken coop. His troopers trailed right after him. The sounds of men screaming, artillery explosions, gunfire, and the terrifying rebel yell filled the air.

The captain came around the side of the front of the house and paused, surveying the thoroughfare before him. There were Confederates at the end of the street, maybe 150 yards away. They were calmly shooting at the panicked soldiers who tried to run from them. The dirt lane was dotted with fallen blue-coats, dead and wounded horses, and the litter from a disintegrating army.

"We've got to cross this boulevard, because we can not travel down it," announced Captain Orr to his panting followers. "Here is what I propose we do. Are you listening?" The boys all nodded, their mouths open, their eyes wide. "We'll race across, two at a time." The ex-lawyer pointed to a hole in the board fence on the other side of the road. "Head for that hole." He looked at his men closely, "Are there any questions?" They shook their heads. "Alright, follow me."

Captain Orr tapped his first sergeant on the shoulder and ordered, "Joe, send them across, two at a time. Got that?"

"Will do, Captain, two at a time."

"Excellent." Orr pointed to Sam. "You and me will go first. Are you ready?" Sam swallowed and nodded, no one was going to say that he was afraid. The officer jumped up and sprinted across the street, jumped over a dead horse, and a broken box of hardtack. The boy was astonished at how fast the man could move, but quickly chased after him.

Bullets zipped past, and the rebels howled at them, but the two made it across the street and dove through the hole in the fence, landing safely on the other side.

"Ah, of all the damned things to land in," cursed Orr. They found themselves in a muddy pigsty, and had dove into the hogs' muck. The Hoosiers were covered with gobs of the smelly stuff. Ben wiped the gook from his forehead and then stood up. "Guess we are going to look like a mess," complained the officer, who usually was the regiment's example of perfect dress and cleanliness.

Two other Hoosiers squirmed through the hole in the fence and fell into the muck. They swore as they crawled out of the mud, but looked about, happy to have survived the street crossing. Then, only one young soldier came through the fence. He muttered that the other had been shot and lay in the street. For the next few minutes the Indianans came into the pig pen, two by two. Finally, First Sergeant Carder crawled into the mud, the last of the company.

The men made their way through an alley, passing between stables, outhouses, and chicken coops. In time, they reached the end of the passage and had another street to cross. This was a major artery, running north-south, and was jammed with soldiers, all hurrying towards the south.

Just before Captain Orr was going to lead his men into this jam of troops and horses, they heard a young woman call. "Yanks." The Hoosiers turned to look and saw a pretty teen-aged girl standing at the back porch of a nearby house. "Would you like something to drink?" she asked.

"Yes, Ma'am," said Orr immediately, and he motioned for his Selma boys to follow. The boys quickly fell in behind their captain. When Captain Orr stopped before the wooden railing of the porch, his small company crowded around. The attractive girl smiled at the soldiers.

"My, but you are the filthiest bunch I've seen today," she said sweetly with a laugh. "But I bet you're just as thirsty and hungry as all the rest."

"Yes, ma'am," answered Orr, "my boys and I fell into a pigsty trying to get away from the rebels." The girl ladled out lemonade from a large pail. Each Hoosier held up his battered tin cup and thanked her.

"You didn't have to tell me that, Captain," she laughed while wrinkling up her nose. "Why, just your smell alone is ample evidence where you've been. It is an easy presumption to say you have been wallowing in hogs' finest droppings." The soldiers laughed with the young woman, enjoying the sound of her voice, and the gaiety of her laughter.

"Captain, would your boys like some pie? Ma and I have been baking most of the morning. We have given all of the bread away already, but I think there still is an apple pie. Would that be okay?" The boys murmured in excitement at the thought of any fresh food, let alone the idea of still-warm apple pie.

"Ma'am, most of my boys have not eaten since before sunrise this morning. I imagine they would be very pleased to share a piece of pie with you. How may we help make your afternoon better?"

"Oh, just drive those horrible rebels away."

"We're doing our very best to do that."

"I know you are, my sweet captain," the girl said with a demure smile. "You just rest here and I will go get the pie. But I have to warn you, it is not all-the-way cooled."

"It will not be a problem, ma'am," said Captain Orr, flashing the girl his best smile, "and if any of my boys complains, I will see that he is flogged within an inch of his worthless life."

"Captain!" she laughed and stepped through the back door. The boys started talking the moment the young woman vanished into the house. The officer cautioned his men to remain on their best behavior and they all nodded, excitedly. Fresh apple pie! They could not believe their good luck.

Later, the men waved good-bye and, after thanking the girl one more time, trailed out after their leader and joined the mob streaming south towards the cemetery at the edge of town. The Selma boys bubbled with delight. They had enjoyed conversation with a witty, and very pretty young lady, drank her freshly made lemonade, and eaten her delicious apple pie. Now this was the stuff that made military life almost bearable.

The beaten Federal army retreated southwards down Baltimore Street, exhaustion having slowed the speed of their flight from running to a mere walk. The horde pressed along the road, hemmed in by the buildings lining both sides. The soldiers were too worn out to think; they just followed the men in front of them.

Baltimore Street reached a junction, with one highway heading due south, and the other trailing off to the southeast. Earlier in the day someone with sense had directed the first soldiers to the southeast, now everyone turned in that direction. Captain Orr observed the change in direction of the flood of weary soldiers and chose to lead his company the same way.

The road climbed a small rise and here, alert officers chopped the crowd up into little groups. As Orr came up to the mounted soldiers he recognized one of the Iron Brigade's adjutants and worked his way towards him. The adjutant pointed Orr towards where the brigade was reforming, beneath several tall trees shading part of the cemetery.

Sam limped along with the rest of the boys following Captain Orr. He entered the cemetery, glancing at a sign stating that shooting was not allowed. An officer from the 19th Indiana saw the small group of Hoosiers and called to Captain Orr. It only took the tired soldiers another couple minutes to reach the collection of Indiana survivors. Bradshaw sank down and leaned up against a white headstone. The youth was asleep within seconds of setting his gear on the ground.

Later that afternoon Colonel Williams gathered the battered regiment around him and formed them into a marching column. Sam was shocked at how small the 19th had become. Captain Orr was the only captain who had survived. He was now second in command of the regiment. Company K numbered just nine, with the Selma boys now being led by First Sergeant Carder.

Sam shuddered as he reflected upon what had happened during the morning's battles, and wondered why he had been lucky enough to have gone through the day without being hurt. He knew Johnny had lost a foot and had been carried to the seminary. Ben was shot in the hand but Sam had no idea what had happened to him. Lieutenant East was dead, and many, many more were missing.

Colonel Williams ordered his boys to follow him and the huge man led them southwards, along the Baltimore Pike for about a quarter of a mile before turning towards the east and climbing up the slopes of a tree-covered hill. Colonel Williams and Captain Orr aligned the shattered regiment so that the men overlooked a pasture and then told the boys to dig entrenchments.

Though the boys were tired, every survivor understood the value of breastworks and immediately began scratching at the clay soil with bayonets, knives, tin cups, and a few shovels. Others gathered logs and stones and piled them onto the growing mounds of dirt. As the evening's sun began to cast long shadows the sweaty Hoosiers ceased their excavations and settled in behind their well-built entrenchments. Pickets were posted and the exhausted soldiers lay down to sleep.

Chapter 11

The Wounded in the Courthouse

Rachel walked right behind her mother, lugging two heavy pails of soup. The night air was heavy with humidity, and stank of gun smoke. She looked at the disaster that had fallen upon her familiar street. Destruction was everywhere. The boulevard was strewn with discarded clothes, filthy blankets, broken knapsacks, cartridge boxes, dead horses, trash, and a few soldiers' bodies.

The overwhelming flood of retreating Yankees had ended several hours ago, to be followed by squads of cautious Confederate soldiers moving from house to house, hunting for hiding blue-coats. Those Yanks they caught were rounded up and marched away, leaving the streets littered with garbage and debris, but empty.

Rachel and her mother reached the courthouse and made their way up the steps and entered the building. This was not the first time that mother and daughter had brought soup to the courthouse, so Rachel knew what horrors lurked within the building.

An hour ago Francis Kendall had handed Rachel a pail of soup and told her to help. Rachel had already seen some wounded soldiers so she thought she knew what she would see inside the courthouse. Oh, but she had been horribly wrong. Even before

Rachel entered the main chamber she knew something was amiss.

As she neared the door a direful ruckus of moans, pleadings, screams, sobs, and whimpering filled her with terror. Then, an appalling odor oozed out the entrance way, a smell so thick it seemed to coat Rachel's clothing with its malodorous layer. She had frozen in the anti-chamber, unable to make herself enter the main room.

"Come, Rachel," her mother had said firmly, "these boys need us, we can't let them down."

"But, Momma, it's so terrible," Rachel had pleaded.

"Yes dear, the good Lord is testing us today. I want you to be brave and follow me. Do not let those poor boys know that you are afraid." Francis looked at her daughter, searching the young woman's eyes for strength. Francis smiled when Rachel took a deep breath and steeled her eyes.

"Yes, Momma. I think I can do this."

"Good, my darling, I knew you could."

Rachel inched towards the main room, readying herself for the terrors she now knew would be worse than anything she had ever seen. Gritting her teeth, Rachel entered the room. The sight made her gasp in shock. The main chamber was filled with mangled, bloody bodies. Rachel looked about, appalled that there were so many she had no way to count. A weary and blood-splattered woman came up to Rachel and snatched the pail from her hands and rushed away. Rachel's mother turned the horror stricken girl around and led her back outside.

Once out of the building, Rachel took several deep breaths, leaned up against a brick wall, and then began to sob. Francis let her daughter cry for several minutes before taking her by the hand and leading her back to the house. By the time the two reached the Kendall home Rachel had finished her tears.

"In an hour we are going to go back there with more soup. Will you be ready to help me?" asked Francis.

Rachel wiped at the last of her tears, straightened her shoulders and nodded. "Yes, Momma, those boys don't have anything. They're helpless without us."

"Good, my darling," Francis said, "now help me cook some more soup."

This time, as Rachel made her way past the wounded soldiers who lay about on the courthouse steps, she knew what she would see. She trembled slightly but treaded right after her mother. They entered the main chamber and a fatigued-faced woman came to them and took their pails of soup.

A grubby hand reached out and latched onto the hem of Rachel's hoop dress. She looked down and saw a young man clinging to her skirt, his wide eyes brimming with tears. Rachel knelt down next to the soldier and smiled. "Hello, there, soldier, what's your name?" she whispered.

The pained youth smiled, his white teeth showing beneath a face blackened by gun smoke and dust. "Danny, ma'am, Danny Worth."

"And where are you from Mister Danny Worth?" asked Rachel, looking into the soldier's eyes.

"I'm from Wisconsin, ma'am."

"Wisconsin?"

"Yes ma'am, Baraboo, Wisconsin. That's just north of Madison. Do you know where that is?"

"No," answered Rachel, "I never paid much attention in geography class. It always was so pointless to worry about places I knew I would never get to see."

"Oh. Well, Baraboo is so beautiful this time of the year. I wish I was there right now."

"Momma," said Rachel quietly, "can I have a wash cloth to clean this poor boy's face?" Within seconds a piece of wet batting was handed to Rachel, the material still warm from the boiling water in which it had been dipped. Rachel began to wipe the young soldier's dirty face. He relaxed his hold on her dress and lay back on the wooden floor.

"You're so kind, ma'am," he sighed.

"You are so brave to be a soldier."

"No, ma'am. I was so scared. When the colonel said for us to charge across that field I thought I was going to faint. But everybody started running, so I did too. I didn't want to be left behind. They started shoot'un, ma'am, and I got shot."

"Oh, that was so brave." By now, Rachel had finished wiping the youth's face and could see his sunburned skin, and the pale fuzz which was growing on his cheeks. Rachel thought this soldier could not be much older than the three she had met this morning. She closed her eyes and wondered what had become of them.

"Rachel," said her mother, "we must be getting back to the house. You tell your friend that you'll be back later."

Danny reached out and grabbed her hand. "Oh, thank you, ma'am," he said. Then, with a look of tremendous loneliness, he pleaded, "Please come back."

Rachel gripped his fist tightly and murmured, "Yes, Danny Worth, I'll come back. And I'll bring you something special to eat."

"Praise the Lord for your kindness." But the soldier would not release his grip on Rachel, and she had to pry her hand loose.

"I'll be back, don't you worry." With that Rachel stood up and backed out of the room, oblivious to the horrors that were present. All she could see was the young soldier's forlorn, puppy-dog eyes.

When they reached the Kendall house Rachel immediately went to work fixing some sandwiches to bring back to the wounded soldier. Her mother watched her closely, not saying anything. Then, when Rachel wrapped up the sandwiches and made to leave the house, Francis stopped her.

"I know your heart has gone out to that poor soldier boy, but you cannot go to the courthouse."

"Why not?"

"It's much too dangerous."

"Why, we were there just 15 minutes ago. It wasn't too dangerous then."

"Rachel, I forbid you to leave this house. There are just too many rebels outside. Only the Lord knows what they will do." Francis went to the window and looked out at a column of Confederate soldiers marching down Baltimore Street. The dirty men were tired and edgy, and cast worried glances towards the sporadic shooting occurring at the south end of the avenue.

Rachel was furious. What was her mother thinking? Just 15 minutes ago she had treated Rachel like an adult and had taken her to help in the courthouse. Now, all of sudden, her mother was treating Rachel like a child. She fumed in anger.

"It's just not fair," she argued. "You're treating me like a baby!"

"No, darling, you are not a baby. That is why I don't want you to leave the house. You are not a little girl, anymore. You are grown up, and a pretty, young woman. Those soldiers out there, they will notice that."

"Oh."

"Yes, my darling. I know you want to go and help. That is a mature thing to want to do. But there are just too many dangerous men outside."

"But you took me out there."

"Yes, sweetie. I'm 37. I'm old and gray and not much to look at. Those soldier boys don't even see me."

"Oh, Momma, no you're not. There's not a single gray hair anywhere."

"Thank you, darling, but you still cannot go out." Francis ran her slim fingers through her dark hair, "But when the next pots of soup are ready, I would like you to help me."

"Really, Momma?"

"Yes, and I'm sure that boy will still be there."

"Thank you, Momma." Rachel took a deep breath. Though Rachel was unhappy, she found that she could tolerate her mother's restrictions. She helped her mother cut up vegetables and put them into the boiling water. Francis told Rachel of her growing fear that they would soon be running out of food.

Later, once the soup was ready, Rachel and her mother loaded up the pails and made their way back to the courthouse. But things were different now. Two Confederate sentries stood guard outside the doorway and most of the wounded soldiers who had covered the steps and sidewalks were gone. When Francis asked about the missing soldiers one of the guards said that all of the slightly wounded men had been taken away.

Inside the courthouse the horrors continued, though now under the hot lights of gas lamps. Rachel quickly handed over her pail of soup and immediately looked for Danny. She moaned in frustration because he was nowhere to be found. Rachel began to cry, worried that her soldier had been taken away by the rebels. She gave her sandwiches to a hungry hospital steward and then fled from the building.

It was dark by the time she reached her home. Rachel stomped past a squad of rebels who tipped their hats to her, oblivious of their admiration. Rachel raced up the stairs and flung herself down on her bed, wailing in despair. What had happened to her soldier boy?

Later, once Rachel had finished her tears, she sat up and looked over at Annie. Her cousin still slept, the laudanum having knocked the young girl completely out. Rachel shook her head in sadness. Annie was the one who had really suffered a loss today. The rebels had stolen Nutmeg. That mare was the love of Annie's life. Rachel softly stroked her cousin's shoulder and recited part of a poem, "We look before and after, and pine for what is not: Our sincerest laughter with some pain is fraught; Our sweetest songs are those which tell of saddest thought."

A sudden outburst of gunfire broke Rachel's thoughts and she went to the window. She looked down into the Kendall back yard. At first she thought her eyes were playing tricks upon her, but when she stared some more into the shadows created by a dim summer moon, Rachel was convinced there was somebody lurking down there.

Fear surged through her body. She rushed down to the main floor to make sure all the doors were locked. Then she leaned against a wall, her knees trembling. What should she do? Her mother and aunt had gone out again, this time to help the next door neighbor, who had come over, pleading for help. There was nobody in the house except Rachel, Annie, brother Robert, and Rachel's little sister, six-year-old Amy.

When Rachel peered out the front window she saw dozens of soldiers who were lying on the porch, all sleeping, or just sitting quietly. Some were smoking, the glow from their pipes illuminating their tired faces. The rebels had not bothered the house, once they realized there were still people inside, but it was frightening. Rachel had no idea what they were going to do.

Rachel knew the soldiers had been using the privy in the back yard but those fellows made no attempt to hide their intentions. They stomped around to the back of the house, did their business, and then returned to the front porch. But the person she had seen in the shadows was not one of them. No, this soul was hiding, moving about trying not to get caught. Maybe, thought Rachel, he was a Yankee who had been left behind and was trying to stay away from the Confederate patrols. The young girl did not know, and she was too scared to go out and investigate. Plus, her mother had forbidden her to leave the house.

Rachel decided she would wait until her mother and aunt came back. The adults would know what to do. But in the meantime, Rachel made sure every downstairs window was locked, and all the doors barred. She was bound and determined not to let the rebels into the house.

Francis Kendall and Mary Taylor came back not long after the courthouse clock had finished ringing for eleven o'clock. Rachel met them at the door and took the shawls from the two weary sisters. Francis' apron was splattered with dried blood, as were her hands and arms. Rachel's aunt's apron also showed some bloodstains.

"Oh, that pathetic boy," grieved Mary. "That surgeon cut his leg off him, right there on the parlor settee." Mary poured water from a pitcher over her hands, and then dried them with a towel. "And all that brave boy kept saying was how he could never play baseball again. What a pathetic, pathetic thing."

"Yes, well he is lucky to be alive. The doctor tied off that soldier's artery and then cut off his leg. He'll heal and then go home. Yes, he will never play baseball again, but he can still work, love his sweetheart, and raise a family. There are many a poor fellow out there who would give their legs to still be alive and have the chances that he does."

"You're right, Sis. Oh, you're always right. But that was enough for me. I think I'll turn in. It has been a long and very stressful day. Oh, I wish John were here. I miss him so."

"Mary, you don't want him here. The rebels have been rounding up Gettysburg men all day and taking them away. He's safe in Harrisburg, and we're able to take care of ourselves just fine. Now don't you forget that."

"You're right, again, Sis, as always." With that, Mary slowly made her way up the stairs and vanished into the guest room.

"Momma," said Rachel anxiously, "there's somebody hiding in the back."

"Yes, I would imagine so. There's thousands of rebels all over town, now that our boys have retreated up to the Evergreen Cemetery. Why are you telling me this?"

"Momma, I don't think he's a rebel."

"Oh?"

"Yes, he keeps hidden, especially when someone goes back to the privy."

"Then maybe we should check out your suspicions. If he is a Yankee, he might be hurt. Come with me and show me where he's hiding."

Chapter 12

A Soldier Is Rescued

Ben saw the back door open and two figures cautiously move out onto the back porch. The larger silhouette was a woman who moved with assurance. The second was a young girl, who trailed along right behind the older. The weary youth watched them step down from the porch and carefully approach. He froze, both from the pain any movement caused him, and from fear of being discovered.

"I know you're out here," said the woman quietly. "If I wanted to do you harm I'd already have told the rebels on my porch that you were here. Now come on out so I can see you." Ben was surprised at the strength in the woman's voice. She was not afraid of him, and the soldier was also relieved to know that she was not going to turn him in. That is, unless it was a trap.

Ben pondered what to do. If he revealed himself and she turned out to be an enemy, well then the rebs would have him. However, all of the Gettysburg citizens that Ben had met so far had been very friendly. Hopefully she was like that. Plus, his hand hurt him severely and he knew it had to be looked after. He did not want his hand to become infected. If that happened then his not-so-serious wound could become fatal.

"Come on, soldier, where are you?" she asked.

"I'm over here," the boy said weakly. The woman and her young follower immediately turned towards his voice and moved through the shadows. They stopped just a few feet from his hiding place, behind a stack of firewood.

Ben was tired, his hand ached, and he had not eaten since just after they had gotten back from stealing those chickens. Ben shook his head. They had never gotten to eat those chickens, either. Johnny had been carrying them when they went into battle this morning, and when he was wounded, well, there went their dinner. Ben shrugged.

"Come on out," commanded the woman gently. Ben climbed up, his aching muscles complaining with every movement. When he came out into the moonlight the woman whispered, "Good, you are a Yankee. Are you hurt?"

"Yes, ma'am," answered Ben quietly.

"Well then, most hastily, let's get you into the house." Ben did not move when the two women began walking back to the house. When the lady realized he had not, she stopped, turned and looked at him. "Oh, don't worry, there aren't any rebels in the house, and we're not going to tell them either. So, quickly now, come to the house." Ben sighed in relief and followed right after them.

Once they were inside the house and the back door safely locked Ben was led into the kitchen. A gas lamp illuminated the room with its harsh light. The young soldier briefly glanced at the woman but then his vision rested upon the young girl standing at her side. It was at that moment when he recognized her.

"We met you, this morning, by the seminary," he said, gazing at the shadows casting a light across the girl's face.

"What's this, Rachel?"

"Well?"

"Don't you remember, there were three of us: Sam, Johnny, and me. You gave us the last of your lemonade?"

The young girl smiled and nodded. "Yes, there were three of you and we had just a smidgen left in the pitcher." She turned to the woman. "Momma, this morning when Annie and I were at her house we were passing out lemonade to the Yankees as they went by. This soldier and his two friends got the last of what we had."

"And it tasted so fine," added Ben.

"Yes, and then your lieutenant chased you guys back to the line," laughed Rachel. Then she sobered, "Where are your friends?"

"Johnny got hurt right away and they took him to the hospital at the seminary. I don't know what happened to Sam. He was still with me when we were falling back. Then, they got me," Ben said quietly, holding up his hand.

"Oh dear," cried Rachel.

Francis Kendall stepped forward and gently took hold of Ben's arm. "Let's see what you've got," she said assuredly. "Rachel, heat up some water, whatever this young man's got needs to be cleansed." She turned to Ben, "Come with me." She led the teenager to a washstand and sat him down on a wooden chair. Francis then began to unwrap the blood-crusted towel protecting Ben's hand. He winced in pain.

"Ah," said Francis, "I've seen a whole lot worse, today."

"Yeah, that's what every doctor who's seen me has said. They've all told me it was a minor wound and that they didn't have time for me."

"Well, young soldier," announced Francis, "you need go no farther. I will see to it that your wound is properly cared for." Ben groaned when she began dabbing at the dried, blood-caked hand. "Yes, I imagine this will sting a bit, but you just be tough." She continued to wash the clotted blood and soon the stumps of Ben's third and fourth fingers began to bleed again.

"That's good," Francis proclaimed, "let's bleed you a little and get rid of all the poisons." She held Ben's hand and let the fresh blood drip down into a washbasin. "Tell me your name, young man, and where you're from."

"Ma'am, I'm Ben Ellis. I'm from Selma, Indiana," he answered, grimacing at the pain pulsing through his hand.

"Indiana. No, I've never been there. You came a long way to fight in this battle today. For that I thank you."

"We didn't do much, ma'am."

"Oh, I don't know. Only time will tell."

A few minutes later Rachel came into the room carrying a ceramic bowl of steaming water. Francis took some soapy water and then washed Ben's hand another time.

"Rachel, get me some charcoal." The girl immediately went to the fireplace and brought back a blackened chunk. Francis ground up the charcoal and then mixed this with a glob of cream. The woman gently rubbed this mixture over the raw edges of Ben's damaged fingers until the bleeding stopped. She finished her doctoring by wrapping the boy's hand with a clean cloth. By the time she was done he was close to fainting.

"Fix the boy a place to sleep, up in the attic," Francis ordered her daughter. When Rachel had disappeared, her mother said, "Now the best thing for you to do is sleep. I bet you're tired."

Ben nodded slowly, his head fuzzy from the pain flowing from his hand. "Come with me."

Ben followed right after Francis, sluggishly mounting the stairs. By the time they reached the attic he was exhausted and short of breath. The room was lit by a single candle, which flickered its little yellow light. Rachel had rolled out a pallet and covered the ticking with a sheet. She unfolded a blanket next to the sheet and then stood back.

"Rachel, go get a shirt and pair of pants from Burl's room," directed Francis. Rachel nodded and quickly descended the stairs heading for her brother's room. "And Rachel, also bring us a pitcher of water. I imagine Ben will get thirsty."

"Yes, Momma." Rachel was so glad that Burl was not a soldier. No, he was attending a college in Philadelphia, learning to be a lawyer, just like her father. Burl was bigger than Ben but Rachel knew the boy would be happy to get out of his filthy soldier's clothes and into something clean. Rachel also grabbed some cotton drawers and blushed at the thought of Ben putting on her brother's underwear. She guessed that Ben's drawers would also be grubby.

A few moments later, once Rachel and her mother had withdrawn down the stairs, Ben gratefully removed his wool pants. They were crusty from dried mud and clumps of congealed blood. He figured the pants had not been washed in over a month. His drawers were just as dirty, as was his cotton shirt. Ben put on the clean clothes and sank back onto the softness of the cotton mattress. He sighed once, tried to say his nightly prayers but fell asleep even before getting halfway through the Lord's prayer.

Chapter 13

Trouble on the Front Porch

Annie woke up with a monstrous headache. She lay in her bed for several minutes trying to remember why she felt so poorly. Then, just after the courthouse clock rang out six times, Annie recalled what had taken place. The rebels had taken Nutmeg away. Annie wanted to cry but she could not, there were no more tears left. Now all she felt was a burning from deep within her, a fire caused by anger.

Finally, Annie could stay in bed no longer. She quickly arose and dressed. Once downstairs she went into the kitchen, searching for something to drink to wash away the horrible taste in her mouth. Mrs. Kendall had left a coffeepot on top of the cast iron stove. When Annie checked she discovered that the water was cold. She opened the burner door and saw the fire had gone out.

Annie took a poker and stirred the ashes, searching for some embers that were still alive. Luckily, she found some hot coals. She stuffed some kindling on top of the embers and gently blew across them. The coals glowed orange and the kindling began to blacken. Then, after another breath of air, the kindling ignited and began to burn. Annie added some larger pieces of kindling and once they were being consumed by the growing blaze, she dropped in several chunks of coal.

Ten minutes later the thick cast iron stove began to heat up. Annie could not wait for the hot cup of coffee, sweetened with sugar, and laced with cream. She knew that drink would put an end to the fuzz in her mouth, and clear up her bleary vision. The girl smiled when the coffeepot burped for the first time. It would not be long now.

"Why thank you, Annie," said Francis. "That was really nice of you to get the fire started."

"I just couldn't wait any longer."

"How do you feel, sweetie?"

"My head hurts."

"Yes, that's the laudanum working its way through your body. You'll feel better as the day goes on."

"My body may get better but my heart hurts. They didn't have to take Nutmeg from me."

"No, dear, but they did. The good Lord says that there is a good reason for everything."

"Yeah, well it isn't fair. Nutmeg wasn't doing anything wrong. And neither were we. You sent us out there to go get Robert."

"Yes, dear. I did. There was no way I could know that the rebels were so near."

"I hate the rebels. They are all liars and thieves."

"Annie, I don't think too kindly of them either."

"I want them all to go away."

"They will when our army drives them away."

"When will that be? All I saw yesterday was our boys running away like cowards."

"No, Annie, our boys did all they could. Our boys suffered greatly in yesterday's fight."

"But they didn't do any good. You already said the rebels captured our town. I imagine that we are all prisoners, ourselves. What are they going to do to us, drag us back to Virginia, too?" At that, Annie saw a bearded man pass by the side window on his way to the privy. "Who's that?" she shrieked.

"He's probably one of the rebels who spent the night on our front porch."

"They're on the front porch. Well if that don't beat all. What are you going to do?"

"I'm just going to keep the doors and windows locked. They do not seem to want to bother us."

"Yeah right," blared Annie, "they can bust in any time they want."

"No, dear," answered Francis. "I had a talk with those soldiers' officer last night. He promised me that his boys would not bother us. 'Course, he did say they would be using our privy, and warned me that our fence boards would probably get burnt up. But I think they will leave us alone. Just don't unlock the door."

Francis put sugar in two cups and then poured coffee into them. The woman took a sip from one of the cups and smiled, "Annie, you make good coffee." Francis picked up the other cup and made her way towards the stairs. "I'd have you take this up to your mother, but I want to talk to Sis myself. Remember, stay away from the doors."

Annie poured herself some coffee and spooned sugar into the mug. The liquid was too hot, so she let it sit on the table. Annie watched the steam rising from the vessel. Suddenly she heard a thump come from out on the porch. The young girl jerked her head towards the sound, her face flushing with fury.

A second thud made her see red. Annie stood up angrily, knocking her chair over. The teenager stomped out of the kitchen, forgetting her cup of coffee, and stamped across the parlor towards the front door. She grabbed an iron poker from the fireplace and unlocked the door. The enraged girl swung the door open and looked out onto the front porch.

The porch was covered with sleeping troops, each man wrapped up inside a gray wool blanket. A fire smoldered out in the street, not far from the porch steps. A few scraps of fence board lay beside the fire, clear evidence that the Confederates had obtained the wood by tearing down some picket boards from the Kendall's fence.

Annie, her anger and frustration exploding, descended upon the squad of sleeping rebs, yelling and kicking at them. The drowsy soldiers tried to escape her furious kicks. Some of the quicker reacting troops were able to scramble away and escape Annie's wrath, but others could do little other than roll off the porch and fall onto the street. The men lay there, sputtering in astonishment.

A loud barking jarred at Annie. She turned and saw a dog, its teeth bared, poised to attack. The collie came forward, growling in defense of a slow-moving soldier who was tangled up in his blanket. Without thinking, Annie swung her iron poker and struck the dog behind its head. The heavy iron cracked the collie's shoulder bones and it howled in pain as blood welled up over its golden hair. But her anger would not be contained, infuriated she reached back and swung the poker a second time, this time hitting the dog across its muzzle.

Now that Annie's attack was no longer directed against the Confederates one of the quick-thinking soldiers leaped forward and moved in behind her. The muscular boy grabbed Annie by her arms before she could strike the collie again. Another soldier snatched the poker from Annie's hands and waved it in her face, his eyes blazing with rage.

"What'd yah do that fur?" demanded the young reb, his face covered with freckles.

"Let me go!" Annie shrieked. But the Southerner would not release her arms. The Johnnies were all awake now, standing on the porch, or out in the street. The Confederates had quickly overcome their surprise at being ambushed out of their sleep and now that the danger had passed they began to relax.

"Don't hurt her, Willie," one said, stepping up and taking the poker. "She's just a little girl." He smiled at the freckled-face kid and the boy looked down at his feet, face blushing with shame. Some of the other soldiers began to get into the spirit of the adventure. They smiled and chuckled.

"That little girl done boxed all our ears," one declared, picking his dirty hat up from the street and gently putting it back onto his head.

"What you got there, George?" another asked, laughing. "Look's like a feisty bobcat to me." The entire squad gathered around, grinning.

"Hold onto her," a lanky soldier cautioned, "iffen she gets loose she'll wallop us all!"

"Let go of me!" Annie squealed.

The Confederates laughed, but then their joy ended when the one whose collie had been hurt, wailed in distress, "Oh Lordy, look at Shep." The Southerners pushed past Annie and crowded around the injured dog, ignoring the raging girl. Even the boy who was holding Annie's arms pushed her aside and hurried to his friend's side.

The young soldiers knelt around the dog, shocked by the collie's injuries. Many of the soldiers petted the hurt mascot tenderly. In time, a few of the boys turned from the wounded dog and stared up at Annie in surprise and disgust. "Why'd yah do that to Shep?" one of them asked.

Annie looked from soldier to soldier. She could not answer. She was horrified at what she had just done. Oh, there was nothing wrong with rousting out all of the soldiers, kicking and hitting them, but not the collie. Annie's heart began to ache when she realized that her anger had driven her to hurt a dog. And she loved animals so much.

"You've hurt Shep," the young freckled-face youth announced sadly. The Confederates again, crowded around the collie, touching and petting it. The boys gazed at the dog, their eyes filled with tears.

"Shep's been with us since Manassas."

"Yep. He's been our good-luck hound," added another, who gazed up at Annie, tears in his eyes.

"And now you hurt him. Bad." The young Confederates, and there was not one of them who was more than 18 or 19 years old, closed in tightly around their cherished dog. Shep whimpered slightly, a distressed sound that cleaved Annie's soul.

One of the young soldiers began to sob. Huge tears rolled down his dirty cheeks. He stood up and faced away from Annie, a grubby paw covering his mouth. The boy mumbled something sadly and then sat down on the porch step. He looked at the street, shoulders heaving as he cried.

Annie suddenly realized that these fellows huddled around the collie were not dangerous killers, nor had they been any threat to her. In fact, they had not been bothering the Kendall house at all. It was just her own hate which had caused this incident. Annie's anger melted away as she searched the soldiers' homesick eyes, and she suddenly saw them for what they were: just a bunch of boys far from home. They were lonely, homesick, scared, and probably hungry.

Annie guessed that for many this was probably the first time in their life that they had been away from home. She looked at these boys' sunburned faces and imagined they would not be able to give her any eloquent arguments for, or against, slavery. The girl realized these young Confederates had no anger, or hate for her. No, they were hardly older than Annie, herself, and were out on their own, and had probably had little idea about what was going on.

Annie pressed forward and cried, "Let me help!" But the soldiers pushed her away, pleading for her to leave them alone. She backed up, tormented by the ghastliness of her action and began to cry.

"What's going on here?" demanded Francis, marching out onto the porch, her face grim. She saw her niece standing just beyond a cluster of kneeling Confederates who crowded around a bleeding collie.

One of the soldiers heard Francis' commanding voice and stood up, wiped at the moisture seeping from his eyes, and took off his dust-covered hat, "Ma'am, that girl hurt Shep."

"What?"

"Shep's all we got to remind us of home, and that girl hurt him." Francis quickly grasped what had taken place. She scanned the filthy looking Confederates and saw that all of them were just boys, many probably not any older than her own son, Burl. Francis shivered, thinking of him. Thank goodness Burl was not in the army. No, he was safe in school. With a deep breath, Francis gazed at the homesick soldiers. She then turned to Annie, who had backed up against the bricks of the wall, her face pale.

"Annie, what happened?" The girl did not speak but stared at the injured dog.

"Ma'am," pleaded a raw-faced young soldier, "we need to get someone to help Shep?"

Francis blinked her eyes in amazement. In the aftermath of yesterday's horrible battle, when almost every public building in Gettysburg was crammed full of mangled and hurt men, these rebel soldier-boys were worried about their dog. "Son," she said matter-of-factly, "there is nobody better with animals than Annie."

"Her?" the Confederates cried in alarm, staring at Annie in surprise. "But she hurt Shep."

"I'm so sorry," Annie whispered. "I'm so very sorry." She began to cry, her shoulders heaving with each sob.

"Why'd you hurt Shep?" a soldier asked.

"I don't know," answered the distraught young girl, her chest heaving with emotion.

"Why, why'd you do this?" questioned another of the sorrowful rebs. Annie could only shake her head in dismay.

"Well, if you must know," stated Francis, "some of your comrades stole Annie's horse, yesterday."

"But, weren't us."

"No, I would imagine not." Francis dropped her hands to her sides and looked down in sadness. When would the effects of this battle end?

The collie whimpered and tried to raise its head. The soldiers saw their mascot's feeble attempts to rise up and groaned when he slumped back to the porch.

"Ma'am, she hurt Shep bad, real bad," moaned another distraught gray-coat.

"Well, young man," said Francis sternly, "there's not a better vet, anywhere in Adams County than Annie." She studied the group of Southern soldiers. All of them were young, slender, and wiry looking. Their uniforms were worn out, tattered, and patched together in many places. They looked like a bunch of boys on a camping trip. However, out in the street, the soldiers' rifles were stacked, with many leather accoutrements hanging from the stacks. Francis noticed that every rifle was in good condition, in fact in much better repair than the boys' clothing.

"Please let me help," pleaded Annie, who crept closer.

One of the young soldiers took off his battered hat and cautiously approached Annie. "Is it true, can you help us?"

"I'm so very sorry," she moaned.

Finally, after a few moments of indecision, the soldiers let Annie kneel down next to Shep. Annie reached out and touched his long, golden hair. The collie tensed, fearing another painful strike. Shep whimpered, and tried to get away from her but she continued to stroke his matted hair and whisper softly. After several minutes the dog began to relax. Then Annie brought her hand to Shep's nose and let him smell her fingers. The collie looked up at her with its dark, liquid eyes, and then licked Annie's hand.

"Did you see that?" asked the freckled-faced reb. "He forgives her. How can he do that after what's she done?"

"Oh please, let me make it up to you. Please, let me take care of him?" begged Annie.

"Can we trust her?" asked a thin reb, while scratching at some lice.

"Well," said Shep's master, "I don't know." Annie looked up at the soldier and gazed into his blue eyes. The boy was not much older than 16 or 17. His hair was long and had a natural curl to it. He wore a homespun brown coat and patched, blue trousers. The Confederate's boots were worn out and badly scuffed. The boy stroked the collie's long golden hair with huge, calloused hands that were as gentle as a mother with her tiny baby. Annie smiled at him.

Just then an officer in a gray uniform rode up and halted next to the porch. "You boys from the Fourth Georgia?" he called out. When they nodded, the officer pointed towards the south with a gloved hand and said, "You're supposed to fall in down at the next corner. Do it now, at the double quick."

The boys looked at the officer, at Annie, and then back down to their injured mascot. "I gave y'all an order, now move it!" shouted the officer. Each Confederate gently petted Shep one more time and whispered quiet words to the collie. Then each youth gathered up his bedroll, equipment, and rifle, and strolled away, down the street. Within a half minute, only one reb remained: Shep's owner. He hugged his pet, tears streaming from his blue eyes. Then he looked directly at Annie.

"I got ta go, 'cause the capt'en says so. Shep's too hurt, what to keep up. Missy, you got ta take real good care of Shep, you hear. My name's Bobby Mason. I'm with the Fourth Georgia. I'll be back, so don't forget me now." He patted his dog a few more times and then stood up. Shep tried to rise but Annie held him. The collie resisted briefly but then gave himself up to her.

"I will," she answered quietly.

As he gathered up his gear the soldier asked, "What's your name, red?"

"It's Annie Taylor."

"I'll see you again, Miss Annie Taylor," he called out as he jogged after his comrades. "Take real good care of Shep. He's all I got in this, here world."

Annie looked at the soldier as he disappeared down the street and murmured, "Please come back. I will have your Shep healthy for you."

Chapter 14

The Water Detail

By noon the flies were beginning to drive Sam crazy. Lying on his back at the bottom of the regiment's breastworks, he tried to ignore the hundreds of flies descending upon him. Oh, he could overlook the buzzing they made, but not the ticklish touch of their tiny footpads as they skittered about on his face and hands. That was what drove him to insanity. There was no way to stop them. Sam had tried covering his head with his coat but the day was just too hot for that. He discovered that swatting at the elusive creatures was just an exhaustive waste of time. About all he could do was curse at the blasted things. But they would not go away.

"Where's Bradshaw?" called out First Sergeant Carder.

"Here, First Sergeant," answered Sam, sitting up.

"Get on over here, I've got a job for you."

Sam rose up and slowly made his way to where Carder had taken up residence. The big NCO had laid logs and branches up above their ditch works and then stretched a gray canvas tent over the wood, making a wondrous piece of shade. Sam crawled into the shade, blinking his eyes.

"Bradshaw, today, I'm putting you in charge of the company's water detail."

"Me?"

"That's right," replied Carder. "Normally that is a duty for a corporal, but we've only got one corporal left, so I have Joe Helvie acting as my sergeant. So Sam, you're now one of my brevet corporals. As you can probably guess, the other brevet is Jake Bush." Sam looked over at the other rifleman who was sitting under the shade, next to Helvie. The muscular farm boy, Jake, sat there, frowning at having just learned he now had added responsibilities.

"Okay," said Sam uneasily.

"Sam, take the squad of Bowen, Wasson, and Moore, gather up all of our company's canteens, and get them filled. Jake's squad will hold the company's position on the line."

"Where are we supposed to go?" asked a pensive Sam. He looked through the shooting hole that Carder had constructed, searching for the distant Confederate sharpshooters who had been taking potshots at them all morning. Sam could not see any, but he knew they were there.

"Head back to the road and then turn south. There's supposed to be a farm down that road a couple hundred yards, or maybe farther. It's supposed to have a good well. And lots of water." The first sergeant scratched at his dirty beard and added, "Can you do it?"

"Uh-huh."

"Good, gather up the canteens. Don't take too long 'cause one never knows what could happen. Sam, we need those canteens filled, and back here quickly. Good luck."

The rest of the boys in the company had been listening in on Carder's conversation and knew who would be accompanying Sam. The other three—Sam Bowen, Alex Wasson, and Ben Moore—did not wait for Sam to say anything. The three just collected everyone's canteens and shouldered their muskets. The four crept from the trench and scampered across an open area before getting to the safety of a redoubt built for some artillery pieces.

Sam led them past the battery and down the side of the hill beyond where the regiment had spent the night. The Yanks soon came to the Baltimore Pike. The dusty road was busy with wagons and horsemen. The four walked along the highway's shoulders, staying out of the way of the hurried traffic.

They found the farmhouse, a large, well-built stone structure with a lengthy wooden porch out in front. It was easy to find the well because there was a long line of canteen-carrying soldiers, all patiently waiting their turn. The Hoosiers went to the end of the line. Since they only carried 15 canteens Sam had them all draw sticks to see who would remain in line. He won, and so did Alex. They gave their empty canteens to the other two and then found themselves a shady place to rest, next to the stone walls of a huge barn.

After sitting for a few minutes, Alex said slowly, "That was something, yesterday."

"Yeah."

The sad-faced soldier brought out his pipe and filled the bowl with tobacco. He did this deliberately, just as he did everything. Some of the boys in the company said Alex was a few bales short of a full load, but others just argued that he was never in a hurry. The big farmer did not care, one way or the other, what people thought. He just went about his own business at his own speed—which was very slowly.

"I sure liked Lieutenant East," he slowly drawled out, between puffs on his pipe.

"Yeah, me too."

"Of course, I also liked Sergeant Daughterly, too. He was a smart fellow, going to go places. I'm sad he's fallen."

The two veterans sat quietly for a few minutes, enjoying the cool shade, and the luxury of knowing they were safe from danger here. Sam suddenly found himself drowsy. He closed his eyes. There would be no harm in him taking a short nap right now.

It did not take Sam more than a minute or two before he was asleep. As he lay sleeping the distant sounds of gunfire from the south began to increase. Though Sam was napping his veteran's response to the faraway danger was to tense up. Within a short period of time his subconscious began to assimilate the battle noises and incorporate them into a dream.

Once again the boy was back at the shallow stream where the regiment had been yesterday. The Confederate forces were swarming down upon them, coming from the front and from the left flank, screaming their maniacal rebel yells. Sam's dream slowed down his movements. He could not move his feet because they seemed to get stuck each time he took a step. The rebs were racing to get him and he could not move fast enough to get away. Then Sam saw that Confederate raise his rifle and take aim at him. Sam knew the Johnny was going to shoot but he was frozen. The bullet struck him in the stomach with a terrible blow.

Sam woke up with a jerk. He sat up, his heart pounding, sweat pouring down his forehead. Alex looked at the boy but did not say anything. The farmer just slowly puffed on his pipe. Sam lay back down, letting his heart return to its normal pace. He fingered the deformed spot on his belt buckle, and sighed.

"Ghosts?" said Alex softly.

"I guess so."

"Yep, I get them all the time. I hate them but they are like old friends to me. They come, scare me some, and then go away. Then I know I can sleep the rest of the night in peace."

"I never had any problems before."

"Hmm. Well, Sam, maybe you just been lucky so far. My ghosts have been with me ever since South Mountain."

"South Mountain?"

"Yep. Do you remember that dead Johnny we found who was killed, kneeling behind the stone fence? You know, the one who was shot dead but did not fall down, and just kept kneeling and aiming his rifle?"

"I remember."

"Yep. Well, he visits me on occasion. I can see his eyes glowing red in the dark, and he follows my every movement. I can't never get away from him."

"How does it end?"

"Oh, he shoots me." Alex looked down at his pipe and saw that he had burnt up nearly all of the tobacco. He sighed and knocked the dead embers out. "Don't like it none a'tall. No I don't."

Sam shook his head. He had heard others in the company complain about nightmares and had seen a couple fellows who could not go to sleep until they had some whiskey, but he thought they were just worryworts. In fact, last night was a good example of what a bad dream could do. One of the boys was having such a horrible nightmare that he yelled out in his sleep, "Here they come!"

This frightened cry was so dramatic that one of the pickets, who was dozing, grabbed his rifle and fired it. Within seconds the rest of the night guards, also having heard the shouted warning, began shooting into the darkness. Before anyone could figure out what was happening, almost every rifleman in the regiment was up and shooting, their muzzle blasts, spewing out orange flames with each shot.

The commotion aroused the other regiments in the Iron Brigade and within five minutes the soldiers in the units on each side of the 19th Indiana were also firing blindly into the night. It took the officers nearly a quarter of an hour to calm the scared men and stop the shooting. Sam guessed that probably two or three thousand rounds had been fired, all because someone had a nightmare.

"Do they go away?" asked the youth.

"Don't know 'bout yours, there Sammy-boy, but my uncle who was in the Mexican War, he came back from down there with ghosts and would not go to sleep unless my aunt double-checked to make sure every door and window was locked. He used to drive her crazy, what with want'un every window shut up, even in summer time."

Sam shuddered. He stood up and stretched and gazed around at the Pennsylvania landscape. The hill before them rose prominently above the surrounding terrain and then sloped off towards Gettysburg. The heights were covered with tall trees, heavy with the season's foliage. When Sam studied the farm he noticed the barn was huge. The sturdy walls were made of stone. Some regiment's medical officers had set up inside the barn but right now did not have much business. So, most of the surgeons and their assistants were lounging around, talking and smoking cigars.

Sam Bowen and Ben Moore trudged up, loaded down with all of the filled canteens. They handed some to Sam and Wasson and then the four began to make their way back towards the company. The "crump-crump" of cannon fire rumbled across the ground, coming from the south. The steady popping of muskets told the veterans that large numbers of troops were engaged. Something serious was going on, off to their south. The veterans did not know what was happening, nor did they really care. The most important news for them was that they were not being shot at, nor was their regiment racing to become part of the action. The 19th Indiana had already done their share, and had been almost destroyed in the process.

When Sam's water detail reached the company First Sergeant Carder told him that it was his turn to guard the trenches. The other half of the company could now rest. Sam and his little squad totaled half of the company. They would guard their trench for the next four hours, then it would be Jake and his squad's turn. Thus, the two squads spelled each other for the rest of the afternoon, watching and resting.

Happily for the entire regiment, the Confederates did not want their hill, so nothing happened. Oh, there were the pesky sharpshooters who shot at them occasionally, but even they seemed to lose interest as the July sun bore down upon them. But they took no chances, and kept their heads down and did not come out from behind their defenses.

Chapter 15

Rebels at the Door

When Rachel saw the squad of Confederates march up to their house she began to tremble. These rebels looked different from the boys who had spent the night on their porch. These gray-coats were much more serious, and had their pistols drawn. Their knock on the front door was loud and frightening. Rachel looked at Annie and the two cousins stood, frozen in place. Both of their mothers were at the courthouse helping with the wounded. Robert was in the basement, where he had been all day, hiding from the Confederates. He was convinced they would capture him and take him off to prison. There was only little Amy in the house, playing with her doll. And, of course, there was the wounded soldier up in the attic.

"Open this door or I'll break it down!" shouted one of the Confederates.

"Oh dear," moaned Annie. She looked at Rachel with wide eyes.

"I'll do it," said Rachel. She took a deep breath, squared her shoulders, and slowly walked to the door. Rachel unlocked the bolt and swung the door open. There were five Confederates standing before her, their weapons held at the ready.

A tall, dark-bearded soldier, his dusty uniform, new and in good condition, glared at Rachel with beady gray eyes. He held a pistol pointed towards her, but when the reb saw her, he put his menacing weapon in his holster.

"Good afternoon, ma'am," he said with a slow drawl. "We're here, look'un for Yanks."

"Oh." Rachel's heart began to thump in her chest so loudly she was sure the rebel could hear it beat. He looked past her and saw Annie, and the empty room. Then, the Southerner's vision returned to Rachel and he leered at her.

"Ma'am," he began, "are there any Yankees in your house?"

Suddenly, anger washed over Rachel taking away her fear. What right did this man have to come barging in on them? Just because his army was winning this battle, that gave him no right to stare at her like he was doing. Her eyes flared in rage but she did not say anything. Momma had always told her not to lie, but if Rachel told the truth, these rebels would haul Ben away to prison.

"Lady, maybe you didn't hear me? I asked you if there are any Yankees in this house."

"Yes, there are!" Rachel blurted out. Annie gasped behind her.

"Well, now, Missy, we're gett'un somewhere."

"Yes, there are Yankees in this house. I'm a Yankee," declared the young girl. "My Cousin Annie's a Yankee. My little sister, Amy, is a Yankee. And my dumb brother, Robert, why he's a Yankee too. Are you going to capture us all and carry us off to prison?"

The four Confederates, standing behind the dark bearded one, all began to chuckle. The tall reb smiled slightly, and then scratched at his curly black beard. "No, ma'am, the colonel, he's not interested in nobody other than Yankee blue-bellies. And I can certainly see you ain't one of them."

"Well, good, your eyesight is fine. Is that all?" Rachel was ready to slam the door shut but the reb did not say anything for a moment.

"Pa," said the young soldier who stood behind the bearded Confederate, "can I ask her if she's got any milk?"

Rachel's eyes flashed from the older man to the young boy who stood just behind his left shoulder. The youth was tall and slender, and had coal-black hair. Even though the summer sun had tanned his pimply face he had the appearance of ill-health. She looked into his eyes and saw sadness, loneliness, and homesickness.

"My boy here, Hank, he's got a stomach malady," said the tall soldier. "He don't seem to be able to keep much down in his gullet. My boy's belly's awful tender-like and don't cotton to vittles of salt pork and hard crackers. Milk is what he needs. Ma'am, you got any milk?" The Confederate's face softened from the harshness of a warrior carrying out orders to that of a loving father, worried about his son's health.

Rachel closed her eyes for a couple seconds. Her heart was still racing from near-panic, and she struggled to maintain her poise and concentration. She opened her eyes and forced herself to smile. "Yes," she said, "we've got some milk." And then to her great surprise, Rachel astounded herself by adding, "When was the last time you sat down at a table and ate, proper?"

The soldiers behind the bearded man mumbled in excitement. "Oh, I reckon it's been some time." He thought for awhile and continued, "Our women, back home, gave us a feast just before we left. But Lordy, that was back in April, in '61."

"Two years ago?"

"Tarnation, I can't believe it's been that long."

"Well, sir," announced Rachel, "we don't have a whole lot, but I think Annie and I can scrape together something for you and your boys."

"Well, that's mighty fine, ma'am. I thank you for your generosity."

"Annie, put some water on the stove, we're going to have company for dinner." Rachel's cousin stood open mouthed for several seconds, not knowing what to do. Then, she nodded and vanished into the kitchen.

Rachel led the way into the parlor. The five rebs followed her awkwardly, their heads revolving back and forth as they studied the room. If the five had just barged into the room as conquerors there would have been no gawking or clumsiness, but instead, Rachel had de-clawed the soldiers by inviting them to eat. She closed and locked the door behind them.

"Boys, put your weapons against the fireplace. Momma would be very unhappy with me if your things scratched the walls." The soldiers meekly set their rifles and pistols on the brick hearth. They also set their leather accoutrements there, as well as bedrolls and hats.

"I don't mean to be forward, sir, but would you please introduce yourself."

His name was Luke Blevins, and his son was simply called Junior. They were all from some place in Georgia, but Rachel could not remember once Luke had told her. The Confederate then introduced the rest of his squad. The boy with a rash on his face was Caleb; the massive farm boy was Oren; and the one that had pox scars on his face was Rich. Rachel smiled at each boy and they stammered "hellos." Then the shy soldiers sheepishly followed Rachel into the kitchen. Annie had put more coal into the stove. "We're out of water," she said.

"Caleb," ordered Luke, "get the young lady some water." He pointed to the two empty kettles sitting on a counter.

"The well's out back," said Rachel sweetly. Caleb grabbed the kettles and bolted out the kitchen door. "There's also a privy out back," she whispered self-consciously, especially after hearing Rich break wind.

Luke gave the embarrassed youth a glare and he looked down at the floorboards. "Excuse me, ma'am," he said quickly and then rushed out of the kitchen, towards the outhouse.

"Rich's got a touch of the runs," said Luke apologetically, "and I don't know how many social graces he's got. He's just a clay-eater from up in the hills. His family's not much more'n poor white trash, but he's a first-rate forager."

When the water had been heated Rachel poured some into a washbasin and commanded the boys to go on the porch and wash up. She handed them a bar of soap and a clean towel. Their eyes grew wide in amazement.

Junior, his blue eyes twinkling in happiness, proclaimed, "I ain't washed my face in close to three weeks."

"I can tell," replied Rachel, laughing at his discomfort. "Now, all of you get outside and clean up. I won't have no filthy hands dirtying up Momma's china." Luke and his four young soldiers quickly took the wash basin out onto the porch, jabbering in elation.

Just as soon as they were outside Annie hissed, "Rachel, what are you doing?"

"I'm going to feed these poor hungry boys."

"But Ben's right upstairs. They might find him."

"No. Mister Blevins seems like a nice man, and I can handle the boys. Just be easygoing and don't put on airs."

"What will your mother say when she comes back and finds you entertaining the enemy?"

"She'll be glad they are not tearing the house apart. Did you see what happened to the Anderson's place. Why the rebels broke all the windows and doors, hauled all the furniture out into the front yard and then busted them up." Rachel paused for a breath of air. "Annie, please. Help me with these boys."

"I will, I will, just please be careful. Remember who they are."

Outside, the boys laughed in delight, happy to be shedding away layers of dirt and grime. When Rachel peeked through the window she could see they were really working at scrubbing their arms, hands, and faces. The clean, sudsy water had now turned to a brown scummy liquid. The sound of the water being tossed onto the garden plants told Rachel that the washing had been completed. Luke and the four boys trailed back into the kitchen, all smiling.

"My, don't you all clean up fine!" Rachel laughed lightly. The boys giggled. Rachel held out a bowl of potatoes and announced, "I need two volunteers to peel these." Caleb and Oren jumped forward and grabbed the bowl out of her hands. Rachel set them up at a counter and gave them knives. The two boys immediately went to work.

"Would you mind bringing in a load of coal?" asked Rachel. "We're almost out."

"Sure," answered Luke. He turned to Rich and Junior and pointed to the coal bin. They moved without another word being said. Luke smiled, "Miss Rachel, I don't think I've ever seen these boys toil at woman's work without as much as a peep. You have cast a spell over them."

Rachel and Annie giggled. "No," said Rachel, "it's just the prospect of properly fixed eat'uns. That's what's doing the magic."

"Yes," surmised Luke. "We've been gone from home for a long time." He blew a breath of air out of his chest in sadness. "I haven't seen my Liza in over two years. She's had to run the farm without me and Junior. And take care of the little ones, too. Life ain't been easy for her neither."

"I wish this war would end," said Annie. She was surprised to hear herself say that, as she had really not given much thought to the war, before this past week. Up until now, all the war had been to her, was boys in blue, speeches, and big military parades with music. It had been exciting at first, seeing the long columns of handsome young boys, waving to them, and having them call out to her.

When the battle had begun it had still been stirring, standing up on top of the theological seminary's cupola and watching the battalions move about. Rachel and Annie had been very impressed when they met General Buford but after that things had become frightening. The drifters who were loitering around her house were scary, as were the close-by explosions, and the horribly wounded soldiers. But it got worse. The rebels captured them and Nutmeg was stolen. Then, the Union army collapsed and ran out of town. The Confederates now controlled Gettysburg and they were everywhere. Why, they even slept on the front porch and used their back yard privy. Now, all Annie wanted to have happen was for them to go away. Suddenly, the war was not an exciting game.

"I miss my Liza very much," said Luke. "I would be happy to call this whole war off and just go home."

"What about the slaves?" asked Rachel. "Would you be willing to free them?"

"Slaves? We don't got any darkies. Me and my family, we're proud of who we are, and our own labor. There ain't going to be no coloreds doing slave work for me. I ain't going to be taking one plug nickel from no darky's sweat."

"But isn't that why you are fighting?"

"No, ma'am, I ain't fighting for no slave. I'ze ah in this here war because there ain't going to be no government what's going to tell me what I can own or not own."

"I thought you all had slaves."

"Oh no, Miss Rachel. Ain't nobody in our company what owns darkies, except the captain and the lieutenant. The rest of us, we all is farmers who work the soil with our own hands."

"So, why don't you just go home?"

"You mean desert?"

"Just walk away and go home."

"I done give that some thought, ma'am. Especially after Sharpsburg, last fall. But I can't do that."

"Why not?"

"Cuz, Miss Rachel, I am beholding to the captain. He and his pappy done helped my family before the war, what when I was a need'un to buy a new team of mules."

"You're staying in the army because of some mules?"

"No, it's more'n that. The Wofford family has always been good to us, buying our hogs at top price, and our corn too. If it weren't for them, why my Liza and I would not have been able to do as well as we have." Luke paused for a moment, touching the thin silver band that was on his ring finger. "My Liza and I figured this would be one way we could say thanks to the Woffords. But then again, we had no idea the war would last so long. We thought it would be over after that fight at Manassas, back in '61. But it ain't."

"No, it's not," replied Rachel softly.

The boys were finished peeling the potatoes, so Rachel and Annie put them into the water to boil. The coal buckets were resupplied so Luke put the boys to cleaning up the mess in the back yard. Rachel was really grateful for that because the back yard had really begun to stink since many of the soldiers who had slept on their porch had not waited to use the outhouse.

Later, little Amy came into the kitchen and saw the Confederates. At first she was afraid of them but soon her inquisitiveness overcame her fear. Amy started playing hide-and-seek with the boys and she giggled loudly whenever they found her. Finally, Amy decided to sing, her sweet young voice, frail and tender. At first she sang Bible study songs, but then, upon the boys' encouragement, sang the "Battle Hymn of the Republic," and finally she got up the courage to sing, "We'll Hang Jeff Davis on a Sour Apple Tree." The happy young men cheered the tiny little blond and Amy flashed them her best smiles, curtsied deeply, and then ran out of the room.

When Rachel announced that dinner was ready the boys all bubbled with anticipation. She directed them to carry the bowls of potatoes and gravy, the fried ham, the biscuits, the fruit, and the green beans to the table. The boys did this woman's work without complaint. Then, they surprised Rachel by all standing at their chairs until Luke had seated her, Annie, and little Amy. Robert had been coaxed out of the basement and sulkingly took his seat at the table. Luke said a thoughtful meal prayer, and then the eating began. Rachel was amazed at how quickly the boys filled their plates, and then emptied them.

The conversation was limited, most of the fellows had little to say. They just kept stuffing food into their mouths. Luke talked some, telling stories of their adventures, though refraining from describing anything having to do with battles.

Once, when the chatting had fallen silent and the only sounds in the dining room were of cutlery against plates, there was a thumping sound which came from upstairs. Rachel froze, frightened because she knew who had made that sound. Luke looked at the ceiling, having heard the noise also, but continued to chew his food.

Then he said, "I think your house just got hit by a stray shell."

"Oh," said both Annie and Rachel, covering their anxious mouths with white linen handkerchiefs.

"I'd almost forgotten there is a battle going on. There has been some heavy fighting going on south of here. It sounds like we're winning again, just like yesterday."

"Oh, dear," gasped Rachel. "I don't want to talk about fighting. Pop always said we could only talk about pleasant things at the dinner table. He said that would be better for our digestion."

"Ma'am, your father is a very wise man. I'm sorry. Where is your father?"

"Oh, he's in Philadelphia. Pop's an attorney and has been there for the past two weeks working on a case. We don't know when he will be back."

"And your older brother and sister?"

"Carrie's in Harrisburg at a finishing school. Momma says I can go there next year, too. Burl's in Harrisburg, too. He's also going to school."

"Such busy people, you Yankees are. And such travelers. You know, I never even got out of Pickens County until I was 16. And even until the war, the farthest I'd ever been was to Atlanta. And now I've been to Virginia, Maryland, and Pennsylvania." Luke paused as he chewed. "Of course now, I would be a whole lot happier iffen I was back home in Jasper right now."

"I'm sure you would be."

"And I bet there's a whole passel of Georgia boys what would be tickled pink to be back home, walking behind the rear end of some smelly, dumb mule." At that the four farm boys all chuckled.

"I'd even be glad to be doing all those chores my pa used to lay on me every day," added Junior.

"Well, maybe this war will end soon," said Annie hopefully, glancing at Rachel when they heard another noise coming from upstairs.

"Once Marse Robert wins this here big battle in Pennsylvania, maybe your Abe Lincoln will see no more point in want'un to continue this here war. It would be grand if he called for a truce and Jeff Davis and him set down and wrote out terms to end this strife. Then we could go home." Everyone sitting at the table agreed that a cessation to the war would be a wondrous thing.

The dinner lasted for another quarter of an hour and by then, nearly all of the food had been consumed. The table was cleared and Luke insisted that his boys do more "woman's work" and wash the dishes. Rachel assented when Junior told her they were not really excited about going back outside. But finally, the dishes were done and Luke and the boys put on their soldiers' equipment.

As they stood at the door Luke handed Rachel a piece of paper on which he had written with a bold hand. The letter informed the reader that this house had been inspected for Yankee deserters and that none had been found. "If anyone else comes to your house, look'un for Yankees, you just show them this note. That should keep you from having anymore uninvited guests."

"Thank-you so much," said Rachel, weakly. Her knees were beginning to buckle from the stress. The Confederates waved good-bye and went out onto the street. Rachel slowly closed the door, locked it, and then sagged down onto the floor, completely exhausted.

"Oh, Rachel," cried Annie, "you were so brave. Entertaining those rebels and all the while, knowing that soldier was hiding upstairs."

"Help me, Annie, I think I might faint." Annie helped Rachel stand up and guided her to a settee, where she reclined in weariness. Annie brought Rachel a cup of coffee but Rachel's hands were trembling so much she spilled the black liquid into the saucer. Annie took the coffee cup away from her cousin and let her rest.

Not long afterwards, Francis and Mary came back from helping at the courthouse. Their aprons were covered with blood, as were their hands and arms. The two tired sisters washed up, changed clothing, and then listened to the story their daughters told them.

Chapter 16

Camp Stories

Ben was awake when Rachel and her mother climbed up into the attic to see how he was doing. The Kendall women had come up early in the morning but the exhausted soldier had been asleep and they did not wake him up. Now, he lay on the pallet staring out the dormer window. The summer sun had heated Ben's top-stairs chamber, so he had opened the window. There was no air moving in the tiny room and the smell of Ben's unwashed body was very strong. The youth had been extremely thirsty all day and had consumed all of the water he had been left with the night before. He also had filled the chamber pot.

Rachel and her mother took the empty pitcher away, as well as the chamber pot. They soon returned with clean clothes, a washbasin, soup, and hot water. When the Kendalls withdrew Ben happily washed, realizing this was his first bath in nearly two weeks. He then put on the clean clothing. When Annie, Rachel, and her mother returned they brought soup, pickles, bread, and a pitcher of milk. The four settled down next to the dormer window and had a picnic.

Ben was amazed when the girls explained to him their story about the visitors for dinner. He told them they were incredibly brave to have been able to entertain the Confederates, knowing that he was hiding, not far above the rebels' heads. The girls tried to laugh his compliments away but both enjoyed his praise. They sat looking at the tanned soldier, now wearing Burl's pants and shirt. Burl's arms were much longer than Ben's, so Francis rolled the sleeves up for the young Indianan.

Francis inspected Ben's hand, washed it clean again, and let it dry in the air. Even though she had tried her best last night, it appeared that his little finger was starting to become infected. The appendage was swollen, hot to the touch, and turning reddish in color. Francis knew the local doctors were way too busy to check on a simple wound of a finger, so she hoped keeping the hand clean, and the young boy's strong constitution would be enough to overcome the infection.

Ben, who had done nothing all day but lay passively by the window, now was very happy to have someone to talk with. However, he was not used to having such an attentive audience, especially two pretty young ladies and their mother. The girls asked him questions about himself and he answered shyly, at first, but soon found out that they were genuinely interested. His answers became more elaborate and detailed, and to his surprise, the more he talked, the more the girls listened.

As Ben was waving his good hand around, in emphasis to one of his stories, Rachel noticed a dark scar on his shoulder. She interrupted him, asking, "What's that on your arm?"

Ben wondered what Rachel was referring to until she pointed to a birdlike picture that could be seen just over his rolled up sleeves. The boy laughed. "Oh, that's a tattoo."

"A tattoo?" Annie asked. "What's that?"

"Haven't you ever seen a tattoo before?" Ben said. She shook her head. Ben rolled up his sleeve, completely exposing a blackish scar outlining an eagle-looking bird.

"You did that to yourself?" Annie asked, cautiously reaching out to touch the marking.

"No, I didn't do it myself. My friend, Henry Williams, he's the one who did it."

"Your friend tattooed you, how?"

"Oh, it was easy. You see, it was February 1862, and we didn't have much to do. We were in northern Virginia at Fort Craig. The rebs weren't doing anything, and neither was our army. So, we had lots of time to just rest up. I did a lot of reading of yellow-back novels, especially when it was raining and we stayed holed up in our tents."

"Uh-huh," encouraged Rachel.

"Yep, well one day Henry brings in his newly bought writing pen, and the nib was extra sharp. We had seen some of the tattoos that an old sergeant had gotten while living with a batch of Delaware Indians, so we decided to see if we could make our own.

"How?"

"Oh, it was actually pretty easy. We used Henry's new pen and poked the skin, just pricking it enough to make a small hole. Then, we added some ink and poked it into the hole. It's pretty first-rate, don't you think?"

"That sounds like the most foolish thing I've ever heard of," said Rachel's mother, frowning at the girls who fawned over the crude depiction of an eagle.

"Yep, that's what Henry's mom said too."

"His mother?"

"Yeah, she and some other ladies came to visit us in camp. When she saw Henry's tattoo, and it was a wonderful looking bear, she became very angry and grabbed Henry by the ear and hauled him out of our tent. She gave him a fierce tongue-lashing that reminded me of when I fouled things up with Pa."

"Well, good for her," stated Francis, "at least Henry's mother knows what is right for her son."

"But that wasn't all," continued Ben, his eyes closed as he thought back to those innocent days of early 1862. "Henry's ma dragged him right up to our captain. That was Captain Sam Williams then, he's our colonel now," Ben interjected. "Well, she pointed her finger in the captain's face and began shaking it violently and yelling at him like he was a little boy."

"That's what I would have done," added Francis.

"Yeah, well Captain Williams, he doesn't know what to do, and Henry's ma won't let him get away. She stands there, looking up at him, and a hollering at him because he let her son get tattooed. The captain's trying to back away but she won't let him escape. He's looking around for help but the lieutenants both run away, and he's all alone, taking her wrath."

"So what happened next?" asked Rachel, a friendly smile on her face.

"Well, there was nothing he could do but apologize a hundred times, and let Henry's ma wail away. So, finally she runs out of steam and crosses her arms and stands before the captain and asks him what is he going to do. Now, Captain Williams, he is a big man in Selma. He's one of our wealthiest farmers, and is used to bossing lots of people around. I don't think he'd been chewed out like that for a long, long time. So, he meekly looks down at Henry's ma and doesn't know what to say. Finally, he asks her if it would be all right if Henry was turned over to the chaplain, to be his assistant, and to help with the Sunday sermons. Well, that makes Henry's ma happy and she leaves the captain alone."

"Well done," admitted Francis.

"So now, she comes looking for us," said Ben, his eyes merry with the happy memory.

"Oh-no," giggled Rachel.

"Yep, well we done seen what Henry's ma did to the captain so we weren't going to stick around for our share of the punishment. Oh, but did we run. But it didn't help much. Henry's ma started a yelling real loud, so loud everyone in the camp could hear her. You could see the boys clearing out and getting away from her, all around. We all ran and hid with the Wisconsin boys. Later Lieutenant East, he came and found us and said it was safe to come back. Lieutenant East told us that Henry's mother had said her good-byes to her boy, and left to go home to Indiana."

"Lieutenant East, is that the handsome officer we talked with yesterday?"

"Yes."

"He seems like a really nice man. And he said that he was your teacher before the war." Rachel smiled, "What happened to him?"

With that, Ben's story ended, and the lights dimmed in his eyes as he remembered he was no longer with his friends. Ben clenched his eyes shut and gritted his teeth, recalling the bullet striking Lieutenant East in the back of his head. The young Hoosier remembered seeing bits of bone and gobs of brain splattering onto the regiment's flag.

"Ma'am," he said slowly, "he was killed yesterday.

"Oh Lord," cried Rachel, "oh, I'm so sorry." That handsome lieutenant, she thought. The rebels had killed him; boys just like the ones that she had fed, not more than an hour ago. How could such sweet boys do such terrible things to each other? Rachel groaned.

Ben took a deep breath. He ached from loneliness. The young soldier missed his friends. He wished to be with them, but no, he was hiding in an attic. Yes, he was wounded, but Ben knew that his beloved company had been completely destroyed. Ben did not know what had become of the rest of his companions, and he wondered what they thought had happened to him.

Just as the courthouse clock began to sound out four, a massive clash of artillery pieces shook the still air. The girls and their mother glanced out of the dormer window, wondering what was happening. Ben realized the cannons were Confederate and were in support of another attack. He peeked out the dormer and saw clouds of gun smoke begin to billow above the low, tree-covered hills to the south of town.

"That's beyond the Evergreen Cemetery," announced Rachel. "What does that mean?"

"I would imagine that's where our flank is anchored," answered Ben, relying on his experience. "The Johnnies are trying to push back our flanks, they're real good at doing that."

"Oh."

"But if I know our boys, they'll be dug in on top of that cemetery and will make the rebs pay."

They listened to the continuous rattle of musketry and the thunder of artillery. Federal cannons also began to reply, directing their shells at the Confederate guns that were just east of town. The Kendall house began to vibrate from the artillery bombardment. An errant shell exploded above Gettysburg, its detonation a sharp crack which ripped through the air. The women gasped and Ben involuntarily ducked. Another stray shell tore through the air and crashed into a house down the street, spewing bricks, dust, and wood splinters.

Ben shuddered. He had been shelled by artillery enough times to know that the actual risk was fairly low, however that did not stop a person from worrying, and shaking. He noticed that his hands had begun to tremble slightly. "Maybe," Ben suggested quietly, "we should go down to the basement until this is over. It might be safer there."

"That is a very good idea," agreed Rachel's mother, who promptly stood up and marched the girls, and Ben, down to the coolness of the stone-lined basement. Once there in the chilly darkness, the civilians and the injured soldier spent the rest of the afternoon.

Chapter 17

Inside the Breastworks

Sam trembled as he listened to the thunderous noise from massed artillery shooting. He did not want to have to leave the safety of these trenches and go back into battle. He glanced around at the rest of his comrades. Their faces were pale and their teeth clenched. It was fairly obvious that no one was happy about the idea of having to go back down the hill and fight.

The sounds of cannon fire rumbled across the hills. The Confederate guns were north and east of the Hoosiers' position, and were directing their fire towards the Union troops who were near the cemetery. Thus, the reb shells thundered over their trench and impacted a half-mile away.

Sam shivered as each projectile screamed past, overhead. He knew from having endured the shelling at Fredericksburg, and at Fitzhugh's Crossing, that the Southern gunners were often lax in the setting of their fuses. There were many times that derelict shells would explode, far from where the Confederates wanted their ordnance to land.

"What do you think?" Sam asked grimly, glancing over at Corporal Joe Helvie, the company's acting sergeant.

"Those boys over on that cemetery hill are having a devil of a time."

"Do you think the Johnnies will attack?"

"Does Bobby Lee ever wait to see what we will do? I don't believe he does. Yep, Sam-the-man, I would bet my last silver dollar that we're going to see some rebs going against that position."

"What about here?"

"Hah! Them come up the ravine below us? If they do, Sam-the-man, they'll pay for it dearly. We may be short on numbers but we don't lack in courage. If Bobby Lee wants to send his tigers from down there," Helvie pointed down the steep ravine, "to up here, why we'll send many a good boy to his grave."

Just then a badly fused shell detonated about 50 yards straight up, above them. The clap of man-made thunder rocked the boys, causing them to flinch. Everyone looked about, wide-eyed, and then watched the white blossom of smoke float away.

"Too close, too close," muttered Helvie angrily.

"Stay loose, boys," called out Colonel Williams, his strong voice easily carrying out over the small regiment. "They're not after us, so just take it easy."

"They may not be after us, Colonel," a spirited Hoosier spat out loudly, "but what worries me is, they just ain't very good shots!"

Williams laughed loudly, a comforting sound amid the threatening rumble of artillery. "Billy, don't you worry, they couldn't get you even if they had a firing squad."

The explosions echoed across the small valley and wafted among them in thick pulsations, almost like a gusting wind. Sam stayed as deep in the rifle trench as he could, sitting with his back against the earthen wall. He covered his ears with his hands, and huddled quietly, his eyes tightly closed.

The colonel's comment about a firing squad was supposed to be funny but it touched a raw nerve within

Sam's heart. He remembered back three weeks to June 12th. The regiment had been marching all morning, northwards along a dusty road, but was then halted and the men were told they were going to witness an execution. The regiment was lined up, and the Wisconsin regiments formed nearby, also to view the melancholy spectacle.

The prisoner's name was Johnny Woods. Sam knew of him, because he was a boy in Company F. It was pretty common knowledge that Johnny just was not cut out to be a soldier. Oh, he was alright for drill and marching, but when the Confederates started to shoot the boy would get scared and run away. Every regiment had fellows like him; ones who were just not suited for the rigors of battle.

Sam had heard that Johnny deserted during the battle of Antietam. Now, that fight had been a disaster for the 19th Indiana, and every Hoosier in the regiment had finally turned tail and run. The officers had written in their reports that the 19th retreated quickly to a better position, but the riflemen really knew what had happened—everyone skedaddled. It was the only sensible thing to do, run away and re-organize at another position. However, Johnny did not stop running. No, he just kept going and finally was stopped by the provost marshals, miles away from the brigade.

The provosts brought Johnny back to the regiment and he was taken in quietly because the officers needed every man they could get. But Johnny just was not any good. He disappeared again during the next fight, outside of Fredericksburg, and again was caught by the provosts and hauled back to the regiment. By now Williams was colonel and realized that Johnny did not have the backbone to stand and fight, so he detailed the boy to guard some rebel prisoners.

Guarding prisoners seemed like just the job for a man who did not have the stomach for battle, but Johnny did not want any part of that, either. Instead, the boy found a rebel who was about the same size as he, and traded uniforms with the prisoner. Then, Johnny fell in line with the Confederate prisoners and was prepared to be marched away. Unfortunately, Johnny was even dumber than he was brave. As he was being led to a prisoner holding pen he recognized some acquaintances from one of the Wisconsin regiments, and waved to them. Those boys told the provost that Johnny was a deserter and again, the boy was hauled back to the regiment.

Then the general found out about Johnny and the lad's situation became serious. He was taken before the brigade lawyers and found guilty of three charges of desertion. General Solomon Meredith, who now commanded the Iron Brigade, was furious. He argued that an example must be made, before others got the idea that running away was okay. Meredith demanded that the boy be shot. The division general approved the request, and June 12th was set as the date.

Once the brigade was all lined up, Johnny was marched forward into an open space in front of the men. He was set down on top of his coffin, right next to a freshly dug hole which would soon be his grave. Everyone kept looking around for somebody to ride up and stop the proceedings, while the boy was blindfolded and the chaplain prayed over him.

No one wanted the youth to be shot. The soldiers understood the boy's fears, and could accept the fact that he was not able to stick around for the battles. They muttered that there were plenty of jobs which the youth could be assigned, so that he would be able to be useful to the army. But the generals would have none of that logic. They wanted Johnny executed for multiple desertions as a lesson to all.

Sam remembered closing his eyes even before the firing squad took aim on the poor fellow. He was not afraid of seeing a man get shot. Sam had seen plenty of soldiers struck down by bullets, and though he did not like blood, the grisly sights he had seen in two years of war would be no different than what would soon happen to Johnny. But what upset Sam, and all of his comrades, was this death could easily be prevented because it was so unnecessary.

There was no stopping the execution. The commands were given and the unlucky men who had been selected for the firing squad performed their duty, knowing that if they shot the boy correctly, he would not suffer much, as death would be quick. They had heard stories about unwilling firing squads who did such a poor job that they only wounded their target, who then lay screaming while they reloaded. Johnny's executioners did not want that memory. The firing squad shot accurately, killing Johnny instantly.

His body was placed in the coffin and every company was marched by so that the soldiers could see what would happen to a deserter. Most of Sam's friends did not even look at the victim when they were ordered to do so, but just hurried past, anxious to get away. Later, the coffin was put into the ground and the grave filled. Sam shook his head in sadness, recalling that event.

Sam trembled when another artillery round detonated overhead. The noise bashed into the men, causing them to shudder. Then within seconds, another shell exploded, just above the regiment's breastworks. A few men cried in alarm as chunks of iron and steel spewed in all directions. The shock wave from the explosion swept down the trench and blew past Sam, a hot blast of angry air. He huddled tightly against the earthen walls, wanting to get up and run away.

Soldiers began to shout in dismay and Sam looked up to see what had happened. He quickly realized that that explosion had hurt someone. Sam glanced over towards the commotion and saw a soldier being gently lifted out of the trench. The injured man's face and shoulders were covered with blood. Sam could not tell who the victim was but rumors rapidly flashed down the regiment; it was Sergeant Henry Reeves from Company H.

Sam took a deep breath and looked at his trembling hands. Henry was a very popular fellow. Plus, the soldier was one of their better baseball players. Sam could easily recall some monstrous homeruns the muscular farm boy had hit. When the 19th Indiana's team played the other regiments in the Iron Brigade, the other teams' outfielders would always back way-up whenever Henry was batting. Sam watched as the wounded Reeves was placed on a stretcher and quickly carried back from the breastworks.

"Not Henry," commented Ezra Hackman, who leaned against the earthen wall, next to Sam. Ezra, his hair matted with dirt and grime, closed his eyes and shook his head in sadness.

"There's just no end," said Sam.

"No." Ezra flicked his filthy hair out of his eyes and looked over at Sam. "Did you know Henry was part of the whiskey heist?"

"Yep," answered Sam, quietly.

The young soldier thought back to early February 1863, when the regiment was in winter camp. The weather was cold, rainy, and forced the soldiers to just hang around their quarters with little to do. Sam, Ben, Johnny, and three other fellows from the company had built a hut out of logs and covered it with a canvas roof. They waited out the winter, carrying out the work details the officers thought up for them to do. There also was plenty of time to just relax. Ben and Sam read dozens of yellow-backed novels. Johnny and the others enjoyed playing cards.

Besides playing cards and reading, some of the boys would also go to great lengths to acquire alcohol. Though Sam was not much of a drinker, and Ben had virtually no taste for tangle-toe, either, Johnny and the others were continually in the search of liquor. The regimental sutler had barrels of whiskey which could only be sold to the officers, but this did not stop the enlisted men from trying to obtain the liquid.

Johnny, who already had demonstrated his excellence at foraging, was not going to be prevented from getting at the drink. He hatched several plots to break into the sutler's shack, but none seemed to be very successful. Then, one rainy afternoon he burst into their winter hut, elated with excitement. When he had everyone's attention he proudly pulled a hand drill out from beneath his greatcoat. Johnny had a plan and he knew this one would work. He asked for volunteers, saying each person who helped would share in the spoils.

Johnny's proposal was simple, though would require considerable labor. The boys would dig a tunnel from a nearby shack to beneath the sutlery. Then, the miners would dig underneath the store's wooden floorboards. Once having made contact with the floor, Johnny planned to drill through the planks and into the bottom of the wooden whiskey casks. Then the thieves could fill their canteens, plug the barrels for future assaults, and return to their quarters and celebrate.

Ben, who was not interested in getting drunk, quickly shrugged off the idea and went back to reading. Sam listened for a while but then decided that tunneling in the Virginia mud did not appeal to him. He also declined Johnny's offer. But Johnny was not dismayed, and quietly went among his other friends-in-blue and covertly gathered a mining team.

Johnny kept his hut mates fully apprised of their progress, and Sam did find the operation exciting. In fact, he occasionally took a turn down in the hole, mucking out the wet mud and helping push the tunnel towards the sutler's cabin. The digging went quicker than Johnny had anticipated, especially after he got the help of Henry and a couple other boys from Company H. Then, once the sutler's floorboards had been reached, Johnny asked Sam for assistance.

Johnny planned to drill through the planks, and into the barrels on a night when Sam was doing sentry duty. Thus, Bradshaw would ignore the noise their efforts would produce. For this support, the thieves would fill Sam's canteen with tangle-toe and he could join the enjoyment. So, when Company K supplied the night pickets, and Sam was given a post outside the heavily locked sutlery, Johnny led the assault on the whiskey barrels.

Sam did all he was supposed to: ignoring the drilling sounds, and warning the thieves when the corporal-of-the-guard was coming around. However, the noise from beneath the sutlery continued, on and on, and gradually grew louder and louder. Sam was dismayed when he realized the noises were no longer construction sounds, but rather giggles and laughter. It also became much more difficult for Sam to get the thieves to quiet down. Then, when the duty officer suddenly appeared out of the darkness, Sam had no time to forewarn the conspirators.

As soon as Lieutenant East, the night duty officer, heard the strange sounds coming from the sutlery, he braced Sam up against the wall and questioned him as to what was happening. At first Sam acted like he did not know anything, but he was not able to fool his old teacher, especially after all of the tricks Sam had played upon him, back in Selma.

Lieutenant East called for the sergeant-of-the-guard, who this night was Henry Reeves. He reluctantly approached the sutler's shack with his squad of marshals and glanced at Sam, sheepishly. The laughter and commotion coming from beneath the floorboards became very apparent when the sutler unlocked the building and the guards entered. The sounds of the provost marshals' footsteps on the floorboards silenced the liquor pilferers for a few moments, but the thieves were already too intoxicated to keep quiet for very long. The drunken boys soon resumed their giggling.

Lieutenant East demanded to know where the noisemakers had come from but Sam did his best to act innocent. However, the officer was sharp and rapidly concluded that the nearby barber's hut was probably the hideout for the tunnel entrance. He marched his provost guards over to the barber shack and found the tunnel. It only took a couple minutes to extract the inebriated larcenists and take them to the brig. Johnny and his conspirators never implicated Sam, nor did they mention Henry Reeves' name.

Now, thought Sam, it did not matter that Johnny or Henry had been instrumental in the whiskey heist. Johnny was lying in some hospital, probably now captured by the Confederates, and Sergeant Reeves, who had survived all of the dangers of yesterday's fighting, had just now received a very serious head wound.

"Oh," muttered Sam softly as he looked up at the darkening sky, "they're killing us all."

Chapter 18

The Young Heroes

The sounds of heavy gunfire woke Ben from his fretful sleep. The early morning sky was still quite dark and it was not until the courthouse clock rang out with four bell strokes that the young man figured out what time it was. The cannon fire, as well as the rattle of rifle fire, was coming from the south and east. General Lee's Confederates were again assaulting the Union lines. Ben smiled briefly, realizing that yesterday's rebel attacks must have failed, as the Northerners' lines were still just outside of Gettysburg's city limits.

Ben wondered what had happened to the 19th Indiana. Yesterday, Rachel's mother said that she knew two officers from his regiment were in nearby homes. Francis identified Lieutenant Colonel William Dudley, who was being taken care of by the Stahle family. Dudley, who was just a handful of years older than Ben, was a very popular young man, and without a doubt, the regiment's best baseball player. Back in 1861, he had come to the 19th, bringing with him a hundred volunteers from the Richmond, Indiana area. The colonel, Solomon Meredith, made Dudley the captain of Company B.

Captain Dudley had led his company until the battle of Antietam. There, amid the death and confusion, the regiment's commanding officer was killed and Captain

Dudley suddenly became the most senior of the company officers. The young leader was able to regroup the shattered regiment, and fortunately, the Hoosiers had not been called back into battle. Once the Antietam campaign ended, greed and ambition reared its ugly head and much older officers tried to push the captain aside from his precarious position as temporary regimental commander. Once the politics finally ended Sam Williams was promoted to colonel and William Dudley to lieutenant colonel.

William Dudley was quite happy to let Williams lead the regiment, and helped him as the 19th Indiana was rebuilt around the core of surviving soldiers. Williams and Dudley commanded the Hoosiers at Fredericksburg, Fitzhugh's Crossing, and finally, at Gettysburg. However, during the retreat, on July 1, Lieutenant Colonel Dudley picked up the regiment's national flag, and briefly waved it in the air, rallying the Hoosiers to him. A Confederate bullet struck him, crushing his femur and just about ripped his leg in half.

Now, the wounded officer lay in the Stahle house, his life having been saved when Francis Kendall had marched over to the courthouse and demanded that a rebel surgeon take a look at the badly hurt young man. The young man's leg was gone, cut away by that physician's knife, but he was alive. No one knew what the Confederates would do with the one-legged soldier, but for now, he was recuperating.

Besides Lieutenant Colonel Dudley, the other 19th Indiana recovering in a nearby house was Lieutenant Lew Yeatman. Ben did not know much about the officer, other than he was from Company D, and was not very tall. Ben had only one dealing with Lieutenant Yeatman, when the officer had been officer of the day, and Ben a headquarters guard. During that time Ben saw Yeatman as an efficient, though extremely quiet man.

Francis Kendall mentioned that the lieutenant was seriously wounded in the foot. Ben did not remember seeing the officer during the fight, but then again, Company D was way down at the other end of the regimental line. Francis said that the officer had dragged himself all the way to Baltimore Street and was hiding behind a carriage when rebels captured him. They yelled at him to go with them but the exhausted and injured Hoosier was not able to move.

The Confederates began to argue with each other about what to do with Yeatman. At that moment, Francis Kendall's neighbor rushed out and took Yeatman away from them, informing the gray-coats that she would take care of the Yankee. The Southerners, still not able to agree what to do with the incapacitated officer, let the stern woman lead the hobbling officer into her home.

So, thought Ben, there were three Hoosiers hiding in three houses in a row. The girls had told him what they did when the Confederate guards arrived, searching for concealed Yankees. He was amazed at their courage and fortitude. Ben told them how grateful he was and both girls had blushed. Rachel had replied, "Oh, we had to do that, so we did."

Ben told the girls that Lieutenant East had defined their actions as the stuff of heroes: doing what one had to do, even though one was frightened. Lieutenant East had said that heroes were just normal people who carried out the simple things that duty required. He had said that heroes came in all shapes, colors, and sizes, and that no class or age group had a monopoly on heroism. Rachel and Annie had blushed at Ben's words.

But now, Ben trembled as he listened to the heavy gunfire and wondered what was happening. The Kendall house was located in such a manner that Ben could not look towards the southeast, so there was no way he could see what was going on. Thus, he lay back down on his pallet and rested.

Later, Rachel and Annie came up to the attic, bringing some bread, pickles, and slices of ham. The three ate the meal, washing it down with coffee. They sat and talked and the hours slowly went by. The girls' mothers were both over at the courthouse, helping with the wounded. The older women refused to let their daughters go there, so the two teenagers stayed at the Kendall house and whiled away the time talking with their soldier-boy from Indiana. Annie would occasionally leave to go check on Shep, who she fussed over constantly, now that the collie was under her protection.

By the time the courthouse clock struck eleven, the sounds of battle off to the southeast had ceased. The battlefield grew very quiet. Even the sounds of skirmishers dueling with each other began to diminish.

"Is the battle over?" asked Annie.

Ben considered the question and then shook his head. In just about every fight he had been in, the struggle usually ended when the Confederates chased the Union troops from their positions. However, the sounds of the fighting suggested that the reb assault had been a failure. This led Ben to assume that his comrades were holding.

Outside in the street, three stories below where the three hid themselves, the Confederates began to move about in an anxious manner. For the last two days the rebels had been going up and down the street with confident movements, and boasting loudly to any civilians about how they were going to drive the Yankees back to Washington City. But now, the crowing was gone. The Southerners had become unsettled.

Almost immediately after the courthouse clock announced one o'clock two artillery shots rang out across the hushed landscape. Then, moments later, an incredible roar erupted as countless Confederate cannons were discharged. The air pulsated with shock waves, and rumbled with thunder. Shells screamed overhead and impacted among the Union positions near the cemetery. The Kendall house shuddered. The girls gasped in surprise.

"It's all right," said Ben softly, also astonished that the ground was shaking, this far away from where the explosives were landing. He had been shelled before, and knew the terror that came when a person tried to hide as close to the ground as possible. Ben knew how frightening it was to lie on the ground and feel the earth quiver beneath him. The noise was terrifying, as was the thought of being blown to bits. The veteran soldier looked down at his hands and saw them tremble. This would not do, Ben thought, the girls could not see his fright.

A second fusillade of artillery rounds roared overhead, shrieking as they cut through the summer air. They exploded all along the Union line, throwing up clouds of dust and smoke. Shock waves clawed at the trees, stripping leaves from their branches. The ground trembled beneath the pounding.

"What's happening?" asked Annie, her face turning pale. The window sash rattled from the vibrations.

"Are they going to attack again?" queried Rachel, staring out the window at the billowing clouds of dust and smoke.

"Probably," answered Ben, but he had no idea where the assault would come from. He gazed out at the wheat fields and pastures lining both sides of the sturdy wooden fences along Emmitsburg Road. Yesterday the rebels had attacked the Union southern flanks and not driven the Yanks from the field. Last night, and this morning, the Confederates had struck the Yanks' northern positions and that, too, had held. Today, it was possible that General Lee was thinking about an attack on the Union center. Ben looked out at the Federal positions beyond the cemetery. Unless the Confederate guns destroyed the Federal positions along that low ridge beyond the cemetery, the reb infantry would get slaughtered.

Northern artillery pieces began to reply, the guns belching out flame and smoke, first as battery volleys, and then by section, and finally as individuals. The noise from the Union artillery was added to that created by the Southern cannon. Shells screamed in both directions. Some exploded in the air; sharp claps of thunder. But most blew up close to their intended targets, spewing chunks of dirt, rocks, pieces of wood, and occasionally human flesh in all directions.

"Why are they doing this?"

"They want to drive our boys off that ridge," answered Ben, pointing towards the thickest columns of dust and smoke.

"How can anyone survive?" asked Rachel, bringing a fist to her mouth.

Ben closed his eyes and steadied himself with a hand to the wall. The wooden boards vibrated. He remembered those horrible days during the battle of Fredericksburg. The 19th Indiana was trapped on an open field about a thousand yards from a line of low hills. The Confederates had dozens of artillery pieces positioned on that elevated ground and the rebels began to aim their cannons at the Hoosiers.

Even though that frozen December day was over a half year ago, Ben could still hear the shrieks as the shells screamed past him. He had taken shelter in a small gully containing a little creek. The weather was so cold that most of the water in the rivulet was ice. Ben had lain in that icy depression all day, shaking both from fear and cold, as artillery shells exploded nearby, or rumbled overhead.

Now, as the window sash rattled next to Ben's head, he opened his eyes and shyly inspected the two girls who sat next to him. Rachel gazed out the window, a frown on her face. She ran her hand through her shiny black hair and took shallow breaths. Annie, her green eyes darting back and forth, was absentmindedly biting her lips. Neither girl said anything; they just peered out the window at the rising wall of man-made haze.

Ben gritted his teeth when an air bust detonated above the courthouse bell tower. The shock wave smacked against the Kendall house, jarring the walls and shaking the windows. The girls gasped in surprise and jerked away from the window.

The veteran closed his eyes and suddenly thought about one of his schoolboy enemies, Lee Jarnigan. Lee was several years older than Ben, but since they were all in the same classroom, in that small schoolhouse in Selma, Ben could not get away from the larger youth. Lee was a bully, who at times, bothered Ben and his friends. He would throw rocks at Ben, trip him, or even punch him when he was not looking.

When Sam Williams formed the Selma boys into a company, Lee was quick to volunteer. Later, when Ben was able to join he soon found himself in the same squad with his old antagonist. Lee harassed Ben, making fun of his age, and belittling him before the other boys in the unit. There was not much that Ben could do; Lee was older, stronger, and much larger than the younger boy. But finally, Ben was filled with frustration and lashed back at the bigger soldier. Lee laughed at Ben's assault and threw him into the mud.

The harassment continued, though not as often, as some of the older men began to intervene. But Lee's attitude completely changed following the fight at Gainesville. The regiment found itself in a terrific battle with a large number of Confederates. Both sides came towards each other until they were barely 75 yards apart. Then, the men shot at each other for more than an hour. The slaughter was appalling. Once the shooting stopped and the Hoosiers fell back from their position, Lee, his haggard face blackened by smoke and gun powder, walked up to Ben and shook his hand. After that, he never bothered Ben again.

Three and a half months later, during the battle of Fredericksburg, shrapnel from an artillery shell ripped into Lee and he died within minutes.

Ben opened his eyes and shook his head. Artillery was noisy, and terrifying, but seldom dangerous. Lee was the only person Ben could think of who had been killed by Southern cannons. Ben's old nemesis had just been unlucky. In fact, Ben had been lying in the same ditch as Lee, but about 15 feet away. He had heard the chunks of steel zip through the air and thud into the frozen earth all around him. Ben did not even know Lee had been injured, until he heard others crying out in fear, and calling for a hospital steward.

"If our boys keep their heads down, they'll be okay," he said softly. The girls looked at him in surprise. "It's more noisy than dangerous."

"Oh Lordy," cried Rachel, "I don't see how anyone can survive."

Ben started to speak but then put his good hand over his mouth. He had been about to say that a good number of the soldiers would be killed or wounded simply because they would be in the wrong place at the wrong time. It would not matter if they were standing up, or hiding behind a stone wall. If their luck had run out, well, they would suffer.

More close-by explosions shook the house, causing little avalanches of dust to stream down from the rafters. The windows banged loudly in their mountings, and some of the walls groaned and creaked. Both sides of the valley were ablaze with cannons, the weapons' crews working as rapidly as they were able. The air was choked with dust and smoke, blotting out everyone's vision.

Downstairs, the Confederate dog began to howl in terror. Annie looked away from the man-made storm outside the window and whispered, "Shep, he sounds scared. I think I'd better go take care of him." With that, the girl stood up and quickly made her way out of the attic.

Ben looked at Rachel. She glanced down, shyly, her face blushing. The soldier guessed that she had not been alone with many gentleman callers, as would be expected of young ladies of her station. He peered out of the window, finding himself tongue-tied. Just moments ago they had no problem finding things to talk about, but now, with just the two of them together, Ben could think of nothing to say.

Ben thought of the last time he had been alone with a girl. It had been the night before the Selma company was scheduled to leave for Indianapolis. He was with Rebecca Williams, the daughter of the company's captain. She also had been Ben's neighbor, and friend for years. As the town's celebration went on into the night Rebecca and Ben had suddenly found themselves outside of the Bellefontain Railroad's warehouse, strolling alongside the tracks.

The night's air was hot and muggy, and their clothes stuck to their perspiring bodies. Ben had been amazed at the thrill he got when Rebecca took his hand into hers. Ben was short of breath from the dancing, and surprised by how aware he was that Rebecca was so near to him. He could smell a nearby field's cut hay, the creosote on the railroad ties, and Rebecca. Ben was amazed at how wonderful her scent made him feel. The two said nothing, as they walked slowly along the railroad bed, hand-in-hand.

Then Rebecca stopped walking and pulled Ben to her. She hugged him tightly and quickly whispered into his ear, "Be careful." With that, the wispy maiden kissed him lightly on his lips and then fled towards the warehouse. Ben had called to Rebecca, pleading with her to stop, but he could not catch her. Even though Rebecca's body had been maturing from a skinny fence-rail into a beautiful young woman, she still could outrun him. The tall girl vanished into the swirling crowd of dancers and Ben did not see her again.

Now, thought Ben, he sat alone with another girl. He did not know much about Rachel. Oh, they had talked and talked, whiling away the afternoon and evening hours, yesterday, but still, there was so much to learn. Ben did know, and would never be able to forget the fact that Rachel had saved his life yesterday by her undaunted bravery. He knew the Johnnies would be marching him off to a prison pen if it had not been for her courage.

Ben cleared his throat. Rachel stirred nervously. He glanced at the dark-haired girl and saw the steel in her eyes. Then he giggled.

"What?" she asked.

"Nothing."

"No. What?"

Ben looked at his bandaged hand and turned the wrist slowly. He did not know if he should tell her what he was thinking, and then realized that life was very unpredictable. Only two days ago, he had been worried about what Lieutenant East would think of him being part of a foraging party stealing chickens. Now, it did not matter at all. His old teacher, and the focus of so many schoolhouse pranks, was dead. Ben had to tell her how appreciative he was, and how much her bravery meant to him. The boy looked at Rachel and whispered, "You are a girl with incredible courage."

"Oh."

"Yes. To invite those rebs in, feed them, and entertain them, and all the while knowing if they walked upstairs they would find me."

"Well, I was frightened the whole time. But I just had to do it."

"Yes, and that's what courage is all about. Doing what you have to do, even though you are scared."

"And you too, mister soldier-boy, you have to be brave to face those rebels. That's real courage."

"Maybe so, but I'm always too terrified to run away, so I just stay." He stopped, not knowing what to say, so Ben just smiled. The two giggled.

"You and me, we are two scaredy-cats, but yet we do what has to be done. We're the young heroes of Gettysburg!" Rachel announced.

"Yep, that's us," laughed Ben. "The young heroes of Gettysburg." They both chuckled.

"Too bad Momma doesn't think that way."

"Huh?"

"Yes, she still sees me as her little baby and doesn't trust me to do anything grown-up."

"My mother's the same," admitted Ben. "I guess we are cursed with mothers who don't want us to grow up."

"Why can't they see us as we really are?"

"I don't know." Ben peered out the dormer, detecting a difference in the artillery barrage. "Listen," he commanded. The two looked at each other, silently.

"They're stopping," said Rachel quietly.

"Uh-huh."

"What does that mean?"

"Get ready for an attack." Ben stood up and stared through the window. A slight breeze was pushing at the clouds of dust and gun smoke, but there were too many buildings in the way. The anxious soldier paced for a few moments, and then sat down.

The two sat quietly, gazing out the window. Now that the artillery barrage had ended, the silence was frightening. Then, some distant cannons banged.

"What now?" Rachel asked.

Ben rubbed at his chin with his good hand and shrugged. He was guessing that the Confederates were going to make an attack but there was no way to tell. More artillery erupted.

"I think the Johnnies might be attacking."

"Oh."

The next cannon blasts made Ben shudder. He recognized the ominous hissing noises caused by cannister. The soldier trembled.

"What is it?" Rachel asked, her eyes filled with alarm.

"Cannister."

"What's that?"

Ben shook his head. "There's rebel infantry out there and our boys are firing cannister at them." The young soldier paused, biting his lips. "The gunners are using rounds which are tin cans filled with six pounds of musket balls. When the cannon is fired, the tins burst apart and the balls spray out, just like shotgun pellets, only there's hundreds of musket balls. There's no way to escape if you are caught out in the open."

"Oh."

"I saw cannister used at Bull Run, last year. We destroyed an entire division in 10 minutes. The rebels' lines were swept away." Ben stopped speaking, his eyes closed, remembering the shock of seeing massive Confederate formations dissolve into confusion once the Union gunners had opened fire with cannister. Then, the Iron Brigade had volleyed, killing and wounding the survivors. The remaining Johnnies had fled.

The two listened to the foreboding artillery noises for a few more minutes before the sounds of musketry were added. "The rebels are now within rifle range," stated Ben. He still had not opened his eyes. Rachel watched the agitated soldier. The boy trembled.

"It shouldn't be long now," he said quietly. "There's no way the rebs can withstand both cannister and musketry. They've got to be caught out in the open and getting slaughtered. It's going to be a disaster for them."

Then Ben opened his brown eyes and looked at Rachel, his face flushed. "We're going to hold. We're going to win. That means our sacrifices won't have been wasted."

"Praise the Lord."

Already, the two could hear that the battle noises were beginning to diminish. Ben smiled. "Hear that? We've won. Ole Bobby Lee tried to take our center and he's failed. That means we're going to win. General Lee will have to fall back, go back to Virginia, maybe even surrender if we can catch him before he crosses the Potomac."

Ben reached out and hugged Rachel, surprising her. "If we can destroy Lee's army before he gets back to Virginia, why the war could end!"

"Oh, that would be so wonderful!"

Author's Note

Young Heroes of Gettysburg is a work of fiction. As far as I know there was no Ben Ellis, Sam Bradshaw, Johnny Baker, Annie Taylor, or Rachel Kendall who came together and met at Gettysburg. There were, however, hundreds, maybe thousands of young teenagers who participated in some manner during America's most famous Civil War battle. Having now said that my five main characters are but creations of my fertile imagination, I must state that nearly everything that has been depicted in this story actually did happen.

There was a 19th Indiana Infantry, and this regiment did fight at Gettysburg on July 1, 1863. The 19th Indiana had been in existence for two years, and by July 1863 totaled approximately three hundred veterans. The formation's commander was Colonel Samuel Williams, a 32-year-old farmer/businessman from Selma, Indiana, as well as husband and father of six children. There was a Company K. This unit was led by Captain William Orr, a 24-year-old lawyer, and the ex-teacher, 24-year-old Second Lieutenant Crockett East.

There also were a number of young teenagers who had joined the ranks of the 19th Indiana Infantry. One of these youths was William Roby Moore, a 16-year-old blacksmith from Selma, Indiana. Fortunately for us, Moore wrote several journals, both during the war, and afterwards, and these writings are available for historians to investigate.

William Roby Moore was able to join Captain Sam Williams' company because they were neighbors before the war, and Sam Williams promised to watch over the underaged youth. Moore wrote excitedly of his first days in uniform, "I [was] guilty of letting some real 'pirty' girls kiss me smack upon the lips." Two years later, as the regiment marched towards Gettysburg, Private Moore was a veteran, and a survivor of seven battles. He also had been very fortunate in these fights, and had never been injured.

However, while the 19th Indiana retreated from their first battle line on that hot July afternoon, young Moore did pick up one of the regiment's flags. Roby Moore wrote afterwards, "I nearly always felt upon going into a battle that I would come out of it alright. But now it was different. I felt certain that I would be hit." Indeed, the young soldier was, suffering a wound resulting in the loss of three fingers.

The wounded Roby Moore was ordered to the rear and he searched fruitlessly for medical attention. Moore was turned away, or ignored by surgeons at the Lutheran Seminary, the Gettysburg railroad depot, and at the Adams County Courthouse. The young soldier, now fatigued by loss of blood, thirst, and hunger, eventually found himself a hiding place beneath one of the courthouse benches and slept until evening. Then, once it was dark he left the building, slipped past Confederate patrols, and eventually was rescued by a Gettysburg family. The young soldier's injury was cleaned, and Francis Buehler and her daughter protected him. Roby Moore wrote of the encounter, that he "stayed with the Buehler's for two days, cheered by their hospitality and enjoying the company of the Buehler's pretty daughter."

Once the battle ended, Moore returned to the 19th Indiana, was sent to a hospital, endured corrective surgery, and was then sent back to Indiana. After the war, the one-handed veteran worked for the railroad as a clerk. Later, he traveled to San Diego, California and retired there. William Roby Moore passed into history at the age of 81, in 1926.

Roby Moore was not the only underage youth in the 19th Indiana. The Hoosier regiment had many, including 15-year-old Milton Jacobs, 16-year-old William Hill, and 17-year-old Sam Bradbury. There were undoubtedly more young men who were younger than 18 when they entered the 19th. These youths lied about their age and eager recruiting officers, anxious to fill their muster rolls, were not fastidious in their record keeping. They believed that a fellow was qualified to enlist if he was strong enough to shoulder a musket.

Another young Indianan was Abraham Buckles, who grew up near Muncie, Indiana. Buckles, the son of a Baptist minister, joined Company E and stood side-by-side Roby Moore in all of the regiment's battles. Abraham Buckles also picked up a flag during the 19th's retreat on July 1 and was shot in the shoulder. Buckles recovered from this wound and in May 1864 was injured a second time, while again carrying the regiment's colors. The hardy youth was rehabilitated from this chest wound and returned to the regiment in time to be hurt a third time. The damage this time resulted in him losing a leg, and being discharged from the military.

The veteran became a lawyer and practiced law in Muncie and eventually was awarded the Congressional Medal of Honor, the only soldier in the 19th Indiana to be so honored. Buckles moved to San Francisco, became a California superior court judge, and died in 1915, age 69.

Little is known about Crockett East, one of our main characters' company officers. Governmental census records indicate that the East family was wealthy and owned a large estate not far from Selma. Crockett East was listed both as a farmer and as a teacher. The educator was old enough to have taught Roby Moore and his friends: William Level and Andy Knapp, as well as Samuel Williams' oldest daughter, Lurena. Crockett East was struck by a bullet on July 1, trying to roll the flag up so that no one else would be hurt carrying that dangerous banner. East's wound was instantly fatal, and four days later, once the battle was over, his body had "swollen so badly that he could be identified only by his chevrons."

Roby Moore's two best friends, William Level and Andy Knapp, both marched towards Gettysburg with him. Moore records that he dreamt about William Level's injury and did carry all of their gear because of that nightmare. Moore's journal also notes that Level "was the very first man to fall," and regimental records reveal he was wounded in the lower leg. Moore's other friend, Andy Knapp, was a young blacksmith in Selma. Knapp survived the battle of Gettysburg; however, almost a year later, on June 18, 1864, Knapp was seriously wounded outside of Petersburg. He recovered and finished the war in the army, returned to Indiana, and then his trail vanishes into history.

Thus, *Young Heroes at Gettysburg* follows the lives of Moore, Knapp, and Level, and recreates some of their adventures. The three young soldiers did have a lot of fun during the winter of 1861-62. Moore described himself as "becoming a yellow-back novel fiend." The Selma blacksmith also described the tattooing incident and wrote that his friend's mother "did not like it very well."

The episode of drilling beneath the sutler's store in pursuit of the officers' liquor did happen during the winter of 1862-63. The young soldier wrote, "I was at guard duty at the commissary stores in which were included quantities of whiskey in barrels. Some of the boys got the opportunity and crawled underneath the floor and tapped a barrel and caught the runoff in tin cups and got drunk."

Even though the young troopers did find time to have fun and to get into innocent trouble, sadly, other teenagers made serious mistakes resulting in horrible consequences. The execution of one 19-year-old Indiana boy did occur. John Woods was found guilty on three accounts of desertion and was sentenced to be "shot to death." One young Hoosier recalled, "At 2 p.m. we were halted to witness the execution of a deserter . . . He seated himself on his coffin without a tremor and died without a struggle."

But the soldiers were not the only ones affected by the battle of Gettysburg. The townspeople of that small town were also involved. Though Annie Taylor and Rachel Kendall were created by keystrokes on my computer, there were young girls whose lives paralleled theirs. The first of these young women lived near the Lutheran Theological Seminary, which became the focus for both armies on that first day of the battle.

Emanuel Ziegler was a steward at the seminary, and lived on the grounds with his wife and six children. One of Ziegler's daughters, Lydia Ziegler, wrote in her memoirs about the start of the battle, noting that there was "an ominous sound heard that struck terror to the hearts of all." Lydia also ventured into the seminary building and described what she saw, writing, "It was a ghastly sight to see men lying in pools of blood on the bare floor."

Since participation at the Lutheran Theological Seminary was restricted only to young men, Lydia and her sisters would not have been able to attend. Thus, it is possible that she was educated at the Young Ladies' Seminary, located on the corner of High and Washington Streets. The Young Ladies' Seminary was a finishing school for girls, many whom came from the county's wealthier families. Rebecca Eyster, a widow who also was involved in the Ladies' Union Relief Society, operated the school.

Had Lydia Ziegler been educated at the Young Ladies' Seminary it is very possible the young lady would have known Matilda Pierce, a 14-year-old girl who attended the school. "Tillie," as her friends called her, was the daughter of a successful Gettysburg butcher, and lived on Baltimore Street. The young woman had two older brothers, serving in Pennsylvanian regiments, as well as an older sister.

In *Young Heroes of Gettysburg*, I have Annie Taylor and Rachel Kendall out of school and spending their time at the Taylor's house, near the Lutheran Seminary. This was done so that the girls could meet Ben, Sam, and Johnny, as well as witness the start of the battle. I probably should not have written the story that way, since July 1, 1863 was a Wednesday, and a school day. The girls should have been in school, just like Tillie Pierce, who was in class. The 14-year-old Gettysburg girl wrote that once the sounds of battle began to reach their school, her teacher said, "Children, run home as quickly as you can."

Once freed from her classroom, Tillie Pierce, whose adventuresome spirit would not be denied, roamed about Gettysburg, taking in the sights as her little town was engulfed by war. She watched the flight of Gettysburg's blacks and wrote, "They regard the rebels as having an especial hatred toward them, and believed that if they fell into their hands, annihilation was sure."

Before the Confederates did arrive in Gettysburg, the local citizens got to see the wounded soldiers stagger into town. One young Gettysburg girl, 12-year-old Mary McAllister, viewed her first wounded man and wrote in horror, "The soldier was on a white horse and John [a neighbor] was holding him by the leg. The blood was running down out of the wound over the horse." The wounded man was brought into a house and put on a sofa and the young girl recalled, "I did not know what to do." However, as the number of wounded in town increased and the public buildings became makeshift hospitals, Gettysburg's young boys and women quickly overcame their fears and gave assistance. Daniel Skelly, a young teen wrote, "Miss Julia Culp and I went to the courthouse with buckets of water. Quite a number of townspeople were there doing everything they could."

However, when the Confederates did arrive in town their appearances were frightening to Gettysburg's citizens. Tillie Pierce wrote, "What a horrible sight! . . . clad almost in rage, covered with dust, riding wildly, pell-mell down the hill toward our home!" Catherine Foster, a young woman, scrutinized the Southerners in dismay and remembered, "Their leader [was] hatless, yelling furiously and firing, curdling one's blood."

The first Confederates to reach town battled with the retreating Union troops, and hunted down stragglers. The Southerners also began ransacking unoccupied buildings. Tillie Pierce watched as the townspeoples' horses were stolen, and some of the mounts were taken with citizens on them. One such instance involved a very young boy who was taken, along with the horse he was riding. Tillie's mother, Margaret McCurdy Pierce, intervened and Tillie recalled a soldier saying, "We don't want the boy, you can have him; we are only after the horses."

Once the tide of battle had passed through Gettysburg, a calm descended over the town. It was at this time that squads of rebs went from house to house, searching for hiding Yankees. In most instances, the concealed Federals were discovered and marched away. There also are fascinating moments of human interactions revealing behavior peculiar to the 1860s. One such instance occurred at the David McCreary home. Here, when the Southerners arrived, looking for Yanks, they were invited in for supper. As young Jenny McCreary wrote, "A reasonably social repast was enjoyed by everyone." There also is the story of six-year-old Mary McClean, who impressed her Confederate visitors by singing an impromptu version of "Hang Jeff Davis on a Sour Apple Tree."

Regardless of how many prisoners the Confederates managed to capture, the town of Gettysburg was inundated by thousands of helpless wounded soldiers. Surgeons from both the North and the South worked nonstop to save the injured troopers' lives. The women of the small town also did everything they could to help ease the soldiers' suffering. At first, many of the young girls were shocked by what they saw. One reminisced sadly that "the sight of the men lying on the floor on straw in the clothing they had worn during battle, and the dreadful odor turned me sick and I had to leave [the courthouse] in haste." Tillie Pierce, after viewing a room filled with wounded, remarked, "We were so overcome by the sad and awful spectacle that we hastened back to the house weeping bitterly."

Fortunately, Gettysburg's women, both young and old, had the courage to overcome their fears and soon stepped in and assumed an important role in helping the wounded. Francis Buehler is remembered for saving Lieutenant Colonel William Dudley's life by convincing a Confederate doctor to come to her neighbor's house and operate on the young officer. As one observer wrote, "The wound was still bleeding and exhibiting the initial signs of gangrene." Even young Tillie Pierce noted that she took muslin and linen and "tore [these] into bandages and gave them to the surgeons." There were many Gettysburg women who, as one young woman wrote, "worked until exhausted to alleviate pain and dress the wounds of the injured."

Then, once the battle ended and the two armies marched away, the citizens were left to clean up the mess. The summer's air reeked from the stench of dead horses and putrefying flesh. There were approximately 20,000 wounded soldiers at more than 160 locations though out the region. These men overwhelmed the military and the civilian attempts to render them aid.

Months would pass before the wounded soldiers recovered and moved away. Until that time, as one Civil War historian, Gregory Coco, noted, Gettysburg was "a vast sea of misery." Then, in December 1863 President Abraham Lincoln came to the little town and consecrated a national cemetery in honor of the soldiers' sacrifices. His simple, though eloquent Gettysburg Address gave tribute to these Americans as he declared, "The world will little note, nor long remember what we say here, but it can never forget what they did here."

Bibliography

Alleman, Tillie (Pierce). *At Gettysburg: Or What a Girl Saw and Heard of the Battle.* New York: W. Lake Borland, 1889. Tillie Pierce's memoirs describe how she was affected as the battle unfolded all around her.

Bennett, Gerald R. *Days of Uncertainty and Dread: The Ordeal Endured by the Citizens at Gettysburg.* Littlestown, Pa.: Plank's Suburban Press, Inc., 1997. Bennett documents the effects of the battle upon the citizens of Gettysburg. He includes a wonderful collection of quotes from the townspeople.

Clark, Champ. *Gettysburg: The Confederate High Tide.* Alexandria, Va.: Time Life Books, 1985. Clark summarizes the entire Gettysburg campaign and provides a concise explanation of what occurred before, during, and after the battle.

Coco, Gregory A. *A Vast Sea of Misery.* Gettysburg, Pa.: Thomas Publications, 1988. Coco has put together a detailed description of the numerous hospital locations and added a valuable selection of quotes, both from soldiers and from civilians.

Coddington, Edwin B. *The Gettysburg Campaign: A Study in Command.* Dayton, Ohio: Morningside Bookshop, 1979. Coddington's text will provide a reader with everything they could possibly want to know about the battle, from a brigade, division and corps level.

Frassanito, William A. *Gettysburg: A Journey in Time.* New York, N.Y.: Charles Scribners' Sons, 1985. Frassanito presents a very moving work based upon 1860's period photographs of the Gettysburg area.

Venner, William Thomas. *The 19th Indiana Infantry at Gettysburg: Hoosiers' Courage.* Shippensburg, Pa.: Burd Street Press, 1998. Venner's writings follow the actions of the 19th Indiana, describing the activities of the soldiers in great detail.

Wiley, Bell Irwin. *The Life of Billy Yank: The Common Soldier of the Union.* Baton Rouge, La.: Louisiana State University Press, 1952. Wiley has created a detailed explanation of what life was like for the Federal soldier.